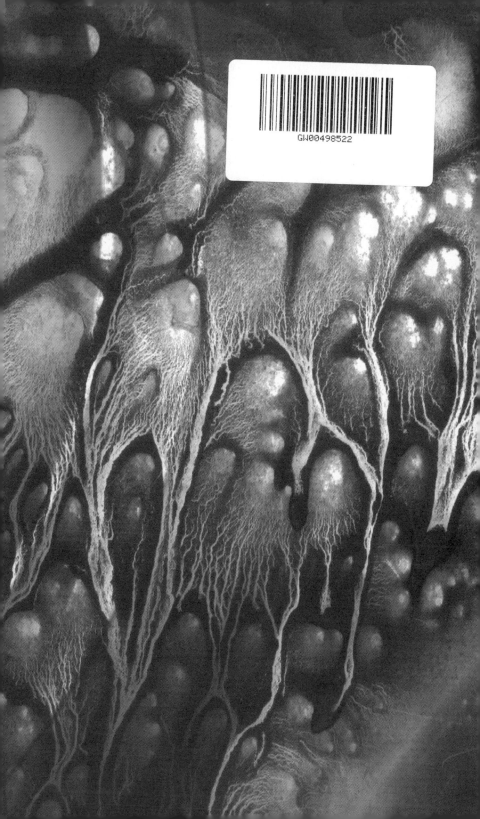

PARADOXIA

Credits:

PARADOXIA
A Predator's Diary
Lydia Lunch
ISBN 1 871592 49 6
First published by
Creation Books, 1997
Copyright © Lydia Lunch 1997
All world rights reserved
Introduction copyright © Hubert Selby Jr 1997
Author profile copyright © Chris Bohn 1997
Editor:
Chris Bohn
All photographs:
J K Potter
End papers:
Harry O Morris
Design:
Bradley Davis, PCP International
A Bondagebest Production

Author's acknowedgements:
Dedicated to those who have withstood the test of my
insanity. Bart D. Frescura, J. G. Thirlwell, Vanessa Skantze,
Emilio Cubeiro, R. Kern & Marcy Blaustein. Thanks to J K
Potter, Hubert Selby Jr, E. M. Cioran and Susan Martin for
endless inspiration.

introduction

In her epigraph (dedication/disclaimer) to her book, Lydia Lunch says: *"No names have been changed to protect the innocent. They're all fucking guilty"*, and I can't help but wonder, does this mean we are all equally innocent? I am not trying to be cute with this speculation, it truly comes from reading this extraordinary book. Those are accustomed to hearing Lydia rant, rave and rail about and against this male-dominated society, in her perception, will be surprised, I believe by her strict adherence to the above lines.

When I started reading the book, I had my loins girded for an attack, an unrelenting onslaught against men. Somewhere along the way I let this guard down, and when I had finished I aware that I had just read a well-written book, and not a vitriolic attack on men, a piece of hateful propaganda. The first paragraph is: *"So twisted by men, a man, my father, that I became like one. Everything I adored about them, they despised in me. Ruthlessness, arrogance, stubbornness, distance and cruelty. A cold calculating nature, immune to all but my own reason. Never able to acknowledge the repercussions of my behaviour. Oblivious to the brutality and selfishness with which I would lacerate others. "* This is a perfect description of this book.

I find this book fascinating from several points of view. For one thing I thoroughly enjoyed reading it, which is unusual as I'm not usually responsive to self-confessional type books. The main, and most important difference between them and this book is the writing. Ms. Lunch does not wallow in self-pity or self-flagellation. The prose is simple and direct, yet never flat or uninteresting. It instantly got my total attention, and kept it. In the end, I so thoroughly enjoyed this book because of the writing and the wonderful sense of balance. In the end there are no victims and thus no perpetrators, which brings me back to my original speculation... are we all, in fact, innocent? As you read this book you will come face to face with certain aspects of yourself you may have avoided and, perhaps, would like to continue to avoid examining. If you have the courage to read this book with an open mind, and an open heart, you will probably have the courage to look a little deeper and more thoroughly within yourself, and perhaps you too will wonder if we are all innocent.

Hubert Selby Jr

PARADOXIA
A PREDATOR'S DIARY

LYDIA LUNCH

No names have been changed to protect the innocent.
They're all fucking guilty.

So twisted by men, a man, my father, that I became like one. Everything I adored about them, they despised in me. Ruthlessness, arrogance, stubbornness, distance and cruelty. A cold calculating nature, immune to all but my own reason. Never able to acknowledge the repercussions of my behaviour. Oblivious to the brutality and selfishness with which I would lacerate others.

Selfish and self-centred, without remorse. An animal driven by instinct. Running on intuition. Always searching for the next tasty morsel, unsuspecting prey, gullible innocent. My goal, rarely to maim or kill, but to satisfy. Myself. If that meant at the expense of someone else's pride, vanity or even existence, so be it. My intentions were always true. To myself.

Days, weeks, months, years spent with nameless faces. Losing myself in anonymity. Both theirs and my own. I'd make up different characters, complete with names to suit my mood. Stella Dora, Lou Harris, Sheila Reeves, Lourdes Vega, Lucy Delgado. I'd stalk bars, clubs, bookstores, public parks, the Emergency Rooms. Seeking to find in lost men a place to lose myself. Searching for a pocket of weakness. Looking for the 'sweet spot'... a small tear in their psychic fabric to feast upon. To hide inside. A place to disappear in, manifesting myself in a multiplicity of personalities which all shared the same goal. To trick the next john into relinquishing his moral, financial, spiritual or physical guard, so that no matter what the outcome, I won. I got what I wanted, whether it was money, drama – or sex. They always gave the most important things freely. Themselves. What they didn't give, I would take.

I've always had a masculine nature. Most men can't stand the competition. It drives them crazy. Insane. Forces them to want to lash out. To dominate, Fight to maintain control. It doesn't work that way with me. It's either a one-two punch, or a fight to the bitter end. The only thing my father ever taught me was to never give up. Never give in. Put up a struggle. Act like a man. And even though as a species, I deplored them, I still found myself both siding with and lashing out against their sex. That battery of emotion which charged my life force acting as conduit to an elevated state.

Lenny grew up on a farm on the outskirts of Kitchner, Ontario, Canada. One of eleven kids. All forced to work long hours tending the fowl. Ran away at fourteen, sick of hard manual labour, the smell of chicken shit. Couldn't stand to answer to anyone. Started hustling pool. Card sharking. Bar room brawling. Got 86'd from every juke joint within a fifty mile radius by the time he was sixteen. Looked for larger fish to fry. Bigger hustle. Joined the army just to get a free ticket out. Pulled a short stint until the dishonourable discharge came through. Began wandering the North-East corridor. Perfecting the art of rip-off. Conman. Short change artist with a passion for check cashing schemes. Fell into door to door sales. Tupperware, Fuller Brush, household cleaning fluids. Bibles. Going door to door would allow him easy access into lonely housewives' frustrated boredom. Sweet talk them. Walk them into the bedroom. The kitchen. The bathroom. Hot hands itchy to molest unwilling flesh. Thrived on their resistance. Their weak protests. Made it a challenge. Get inside them, squirt and flee. Before they knew what hit them. Before they realized they'd been screwed. Duped. Kept a map in his car riddled with little red crosses. A dog marking his territory. Never liked fucking the same woman twice. Bad for business. Never know when the unsuspecting husband might return from work early.

He worked mornings. Spent his afternoons at the racetrack playing the Perfectas. Won enough to cut his losses. What he didn't make back at the track, he'd hustle at the card table. Kept him in pocket change. Met Lucy on a blind date, when her girlfriend Rosalee couldn't get the weekend off from selling fortunes down at the Lakeside Amusement Park. I was conceived on a Saturday night in the back seat of a rundown Chevy. He was drunk, she was in tears. They tied the knot six weeks later. My father's daughter.

I split the '67 Cherry Red Mustang almost in half, flooring the gas, smashing it into the forty foot pine tree, three feet from the front window of the old lady's house. The shock on her face, priceless. Almost gave her a coronary. Al grabbed the wheel. Seconds too late. Screamed at me to back out. Take off. Get the hell out of there before the cops arrived. Pulled me out from behind the wheel. Threw it in reverse and floored it. Surprised that the fucking thing still ran. Pulled into his garage. A couple blocks away. Slammed the door shut. Couldn't stand to even look at me. He had just spent three months and four grand rebuilding the engine. Customizing the paint job. Reupholstering the interior. He should have never let me drive. I had just turned thirteen.

I promised to pay him off in pussy. He turned around. Told me to go home. He'd call me later. Maybe. I shrugged and slunk out. I knew he would. I had him hooked. Hooked on my pussy.

We'd been screwing each other for six months. Seduced him on the front steps of the rectory behind The Holy Redeemer Church. He was taking a short cut on the way back from the Auto Supply Shop. I was smoking a joint. Called him over. I knew who he was. I'd already plowed through half the neighbourhood. The two brothers who lived across the street. Their cousin. The ex-Marine on the corner. The old man who ran the record store. The check-out boy from the local market. The kid who delivered pizza. His older brother. A couple of his friends. Half the guys who picked me up hitch-hiking. The small-time pot dealer.

Praying that one of them, any of them, all of them would help to erase the greasy memory of my father's hot hands. Hands he couldn't keep to himself. Hands that couldn't sit still. Hands that couldn't help but to poke, prod, pinch, pull, pollute. Hands that had a mind of their own. Hands... much like my own.

I learned by example how to hustle, boost, steal, hijack, corral, connive and convince just about anybody of anything. Valuable lessons for which I am grateful. I inherited Lenny's ability to sweet-talk with forked tongue, walk the fine line between obsession and madness, and get what I wanted. When I wanted. Come hell or high water, like Lenny used to say. Before the heart attack killed him. Turned him into ashes. The ghost of a memory whose spirit still haunts, lives and breathes through me. Manifests itself in me. My hands, his devil's workshop. My sex, his unquenchable hunger. A hunger from beyond the grave, which pre-dated my cradle.

The Greyhound pulled into Port Authority. The stinging aroma of fresh urine & stale sweat slaps me in the face after the nine hour-long overnighter. I grabbed the small leather bag that housed all my worldly possessions and shook off the previous sixteen years. I had eighty-two dollars in my pocket and the phone number of a friend's cousin who lived on Bleeker and MacDougal. Sunny was a middle-aged hippy from Woodstock. She sold pot to pay the rent. She said I could stay with her. For three days. Then I'd have to work something else out. I was a liability to her business. I was cocksure enough to believe I'd figure it out. Even sleeping in the subway surrounded by bums and tunnel dwellers would be preferable to spending one more day in Upstate stuck in a ghetto of rednecks, race riots and social retards whose idea of fun was 3.2 kids, the dog, the cat, the car, the truck and a moderate mortgage. I had finally escaped.

That night Sunny suggested I check out Mothers, a club long since closed, on 23rd Street between 7th and 8th Avenue. A funky little club whose clientele consisted of queers, queens, neighbourhood locals, rock musicians and a few left over Glam transvestites. All swilling beer, vodka, bourbon. The occasional joint passed around sweetly perfuming the air, whose undertone itself was sour, sickly.

Targeted the mark. Feminine, long hair, probably from Jersey. After numerous drinks I stuck my hands down his pants. Convinced him to let me crash at his loft, fooled him into believing he'd be rewarded with hot blowjobs administered by my teenage mouth. Played up to his jailbait fantasies. Confessing I had just run away. Broke free from parental prison. It was my first night in town. I was trying to get hooked up. He bought it and brought me over to his place on 24th Street.

A massive storefront. Subdivided into small cubicles. Four other roommates. Hippies and free jazz musicians. Kitty, Lenny Bruce's daughter, had just moved out, leaving vacant a narrow makeshift room, suspended from the ceiling directly facing the front door. I knew I'd have it in a day or two. Screw the dick that brought me there for a few nights, feign my period and move upstairs. It worked. Avoided him whenever possible. Ingratiated myself to the other roommates with a daunting mix of arrogance, humour, innuendo.

The room under mine was occupied by a couple who bore a striking resemblance to John and Yoko, who only surfaced every few days to score heroin or, in desperation, methadone. They gave me the most important information anyone just arriving broke and almost homeless in NYC would need. The phone number of a doctor in the Bronx who freely wrote up scripts for Black Beauties, Percodan and Quaaludes. John and Yoko insisted that if I wanted to turn my now forty-three bucks into two hundred or more, I make an appointment and sweet-talk the good Doc.

I started selling Black Beauties for three bucks a pop in the park between 23rd and 25th on Broadway. I could move my entire stash in a day or two, selling the shit by the handfuls to scaggy street kids who stole or begged enough chump change to eat once or twice a day and get high at least as often. Every few weeks I'd head back up to the Bronx, pay off the doctor, hit the park again. It was easy maintenance. You could get by on three or four dollars a day then, if you knew how. And I still wasn't paying any rent on 24th Street. Only going back to John and Yoko's when I needed to shower or sleep. Sneak in and out.

Hoping they'd forget I was there.

I met "Ill Will" one day while peddling. If Tommy Lee Jones did *Midnight Cowboy*, it would have bred Will. Scuzzy, haggard, a real charmer... He'd bring me coffee, give me a weak smile and ask for twelve Black Beauties. He invited me up to his room at the George Washington Hotel on Lexington near 23rd. A sleazy waystop for local prostitutes, transients and general low-lifes just passing through New York on a whim, on their way from disappointment to disaster. Will claimed to be the only full-time resident. At least for the last three weeks.

The frayed lobby led to a creaky elevator which deposited you on sticky linoleum on a floor you didn't request. It worked when it wanted to. Like the residents. The whole building stunk of death and old age with a strong undercurrent of cheap cologne and Lysol. We took the stairs up two flights, littered with cigarette butts, empty beer cans and the corpses of hundreds of roaches. I needed a shower before we even hit his room.

Room 453 smelled of Bar.B.Q. and old leather. Three black cowboy hats framed the side of the bed, hanging from small nails, hammered in with his boot. A battered acoustic guitar leaned forlornly in the corner, sunlight splashing off the strings. I asked if he played. He shrugged, picked up the beast and sung "I keep a close watch on this heart of mine... I keep my eyes wide open all the time... because you're mine, I walk the line..." A deep baritone, melodious, haunting. His repertoire consisted of Johnny Cash, David Allen Coe and Charlie Feathers. He claimed he could only remember the words when he was high. His memory improved with grass. Asked if I'd like him to turn me on. Had a stick of Mexican skunk. He lit up, sucked down half the joint and passed it over. I didn't know it was laced.

I woke up to another nuclear sunset. The sky bloody pink, casting an eerie incandescence on my pale skin. I was groggy. Naked. Will sucking softly on my toes. Told me to "Git up, we need some libations!" Suggested the Blarney Stone a few blocks away. Made a mean meatloaf. He looked dejected when I told him I didn't eat meat. Assured me we'd find something for "Little Queenie".

I spent the weekend with Will, playing pool, pinball, smoking joints, drinking, popping the occasional Black Beauty. Needed all the fuel we could get. Staying up all night, shooting the shit, running around all over the city. He confiding he was splitting in a day or two. Had been there almost a month. Didn't like to stay in one place for too long. Drifter by trade. Kansas City, St Louis, Portland, Reno, Detroit, San Diego, Trenton, Key West, Atlanta Georgia. He was just passing through. He'd hop a train, bus, ride, walk if he had to. When ya gotta go, you gotta go... Anywhere. Just to get away. Something to do. Forward movement. Momentum. He'd work if he had to. Hustle when necessary. Steal if it came to that. Didn't need much. Kill if felt cornered. Liked me because I didn't ask too many damn questions. I didn't ask him anything. I didn't really care. I concocted my own stories to fill in the blanks. Wasn't hard to figure. I reinvented my life story every time I told it. What he didn't tell me, I didn't need to know. Not yet.

I saw him again two weeks later. On the cover of the *New York Post*. Unshaven, head cocked to one side, black cowboy hat tipped to one eye, smiling. The headline read: "CANNIBAL CAUGHT! CHELSEA HOTEL MURDER MYSTERY SOLVED!" Will had been tracked down to a transient hotel in El Paso, extradited back to NYC and brought in for questioning. A young woman had been murdered, found bound and gagged, her fingers, toes and left cheek chewed off, on or around the first of the month.

Will had blown in on the Amtrack two days before she disappeared. Charges were pending. "Ill Will" still sits in Riker's waiting for an appeal. Trying to sell the rights to his story. Make a helluva Movie of the Week.

Thirty bucks from broke. Headed back up to the shitty little park. Trying to unload some pills. Turn the early shift. Catch the last of the late-night zombies as they stumbled home from The Galaxy or Max's Kansas City. Cross-section of freaks still jacked up on alcohol, pot and coke, not quite ready to give up the high. A Black Beauty or two would give them all the incentive they needed.

Fragile old man waddles up to my bench. Yellow skin and teeth smells like liver damage. Lowers himself down with obvious discomfort. Gives a weak and sickly smile. I force out a fake one. Trying to fabricate the best lie to milk him with. He takes up the initiative to start a conversation. Asks me why I'm so sullen. He doesn't realize I'm looking for a loophole to rip him off through. I lie and tell him I just got kicked out of where I'm staying. Play on his heartstrings. Tell him I'm hungry, homeless.

He offers to buy me a sandwich, some coffee. But, I'd have to go get it, his legs aren't awake yet. I whisper a thank you, swallowing my sarcasm. He pulls out his wallet, fat with twenties. My attitude suddenly improves. He slips me one, asking if I'd be so kind as to bring him back a plain buttered roll, sweet tea. Old man's fodder. Of course. He still doesn't get it. I'll have the rest of that money before the morning's over.

I hit the Korean deli across from the park for coffee, tea and two buttered rolls. Slip the change in my pocket, extracting a few singles for myself. It wasn't necessary. He told me to keep the change. Still chump, I wanted more from him than seventeen bucks. Another hundred was what I was aiming for. Tried to engage me in petty pleasantries. I listen with one ear, still scheming. Wondering if I should just pickpocket him, hit him over the head and run, or plead. I didn't need to think too hard. He piped in with "I could use a little company... if you know what I mean..." He winked at me with a runny yellow eye, crusted at the corner. I suppressed a retch. He suggested we go to the Kenmore, a sleazy, fading hotel a few blocks away. Said he'd pay for me to stay there for a few days, give me money for food, etc, all I had to do was rub him a little "down there". And not to worry, he was very clean... married to the same woman for thirty-five years. *Right, like that means anything,* I mumbled under my breath. It seemed like an easy gig. I agreed.

We took a taxi to the hotel. Grandpa's legs hadn't woken up yet. We were greeted with a sly wink from the desk clerk, a World War II vet with a slight palsy shake. "Morning Judge, Room 322?"

"For two nights, please."

We exited the elevator and passed a couple of teenage huffers sucking glue fumes from dirty paper bags. Cute, broken, skinny boys. Probably runaways from the Midwest. Short shift hustlers. I'd look them up later. They wouldn't be hard to find. Sleeping in the stairwell between tricks. Pray I don't have to join them soon, if the hippies get a wild hair...

We reach the room which grandpa opens with a

little curtsey. Old man acting like a little girl. Awful. The dingy room stinks of violations and stale sex. A faint grey light trickles in through the moth-eaten curtains. The window faces a concrete shaft, two feet deep, six long. I close the curtains. Too depressing. I trace a large X in the dust on the dresser over the drawer holding the bible. Take a deep breath, plant a phoney smile and turn back around to the old man occupying the edge of the droopy bed. He's lost for a few minutes. Can't remember where he's at. No longer in this room. I'm hovering over his flashback, strange how fifty years forward or backward can elapse within a breath's notice. I feel his fear, desperation, frustration. Running from the Nazi soldiers. Hiding in the bush, alongside the train tracks, watching mother, father, siblings being sucked up and consumed into the cattle cars en route to the concentration camp. He was small enough to hide. Run off. Be taken in and shuttled out of the country. Leaving the family's ashes to mingle with millions of other victims who never left the incinerators. Never able to recover from the guilt and shame of sole survivor. Made it to America by the late forties. Worked his way through Law School. Sworn in as Judge three years ago on his sixty-first birthday. Still looking for Justice. Anxious for the peace of Death.

He checks his watch, shakes off the reverie. Apologizes that he's got to go. As if I'd be disappointed. He slips eighty dollars into my hand, asking if he can please be allowed to return in the morning. He's not feeling too good. Gout's acting up again. He kisses my fingers murmuring "I'm sorry, I'm so sorry." Talking to his dreams, not me. I close the door softly. Wait till I hear the elevator descend. Exit looking for the glue boys.

Timmy and Joey blew in to NYC on a Greyhound, like

every other wasted youth who was looking to escape the boredom, abuse and bullshit of family life. They boarded in Springfield Missouri hopped up on No-Doze and Coca Cola, not wanting to miss a single mile separating them and the previous fifteen years. Second cousins divorcing themselves from third generation farmers who watched in desperation as the crops died and the land shrivelled, while days and nights blurred in drunken degeneracy. Sick of the senseless beatings heaped upon them and powerless against their mothers' broken noses, busted arms, bruised ribs, they split. Guilty, at having left behind six sisters who would now bear the brunt not only of battery, but of the sexual abuse that had become a family tradition. They spent their days and nights hustling dirty old men incredibly reminiscent of the fathers, uncles, cousins they were attempting to erase from their own history.

I found them on the landing between the second and third floor. Playing Gin, counting change and rolling Grand Centrals. Nasty cigarettes, hand rolled from butts they'd gather from the ashtrays outside the elevators. Empty soda cans, crumpled potato chip bags and glue tubes scattered in the corners. I plopped down a few steps above them. They didn't even notice. Immersed in a quiet argument about forgotten rules of a stupid card game. Their innocence and stupidity were touching. Homeless, nearly broke, living in stairwells on junk food, none of it mattered. Timmy won the game and expected to claim his half a dollar. They didn't have three bucks between them.

I interrupted and asked if they were hungry, wanted some breakfast or coffee. They said nah, we just ate, kicking the crumpled litter in the far corner with dirty sneakers. "But we could use a few bucks for later..." one of them said, a sneaky smile crusted with old food and nicotine stains. I crumpled up a twenty and threw it at him, bouncing it off his left knee. "Wow, are you rich?" one of them asked, new interest perked. "No, I'm just a better hustler..." Squeezing the last drop from an empty glue tube into a filthy paper bag, they offered me a huff. I passed, getting up to leave and head back to the park. Told them I'd check in on them later. "Cool..." Timmy slobbered, the sweet smell of glue filling the cubby. I climbed over them, using their greasy heads as balancing rods on my way down the stairs. Careful not to touch the grimy rails on my way out.

I hit the park again, trying to move the last of the shit. I had ten Black Beauties left and three weeks to go before I could head back up to the doctor in the Bronx. Waiting for something to give. A sleazy regular, Sal, offered to scoop the lot. Invited me back to a small café he ran next door to the Chelsea Hotel. The menu consisted of falafels, hummus and Turkish coffee. It was little more than a glorified take-out stand with a few tables and chairs stuffed against the wall. Used as a front for something, the ridiculous rent would never be met by nickel and diming it over sandwiches.

I couldn't fucking stand Sal, his awful hair, black and greasy slicked back to cover a bald spot. He always stunk of booze and sex, filthy hands nervously checking front and back pockets, smoothing his oily mane back, grabbing his own ass, running a dirty index over chapped lips. I tolerated him, intrigued by his cohorts from Long Island. Disturbed avant-jazz musicians who'd occasionally play the city, singing songs of basement torture and mutilation set over a back-drop of spastic din. The Night Stalker meets Albert Ayler. Strange brew. I dug it. Sal's the one who set me up with "Ill Will". My short-lived affair with the benign cannibal. When I asked Sal for Will's address at Riker's, he said don't bother. He's in for life plus thirty years. End of subject.

Stalling over a second muddy coffee, when in walk the Long Island Four. A relief from the useless drivel, rude comments, and unwanted advances that were Sal's trademark. The pig just couldn't keep his hands to himself or his trap shut. Just to be a prick, he'd do shit like douse you in the face with beer, just to get a reaction, if he felt you were ignoring him. Which I did to the best of my abilities. Using him to unload pills, for free coffee or his unique acquaintances. I had a crush on the lanky one, the singer, who'd stand behind the drums, towering over, re-telling gruesome tales of kidnapping and forced sodomy. He possessed a strange charm, a slippery smile which would light up the dull pauses between lengthy silences. Sal and the Long Island Four went back fourteen or more years, since their junior high school days. They had little left to chew over except the seedy details of things done and nearly forgotten, whose twisted memories would be shared and refuelled in simple phrases only they could decode. Like "Backseat Booby-trap", "Gin-soaked Gang Bang", "Trial by Titty-torture"; references to their shared escapades of male bonding, female degradation. Cruel bastards for whom I had a soft spot.

They'd just blown in from the Island, taking a room upstairs at the Chelsea. Gina was coming in too, to show off her new tits. She was the only woman they ever mentioned by name. An irritable cunt with a shitty attitude. I detested her immediately, partly because she shared in The Long Island Four's sadistic history of sexual abuse, which until now I'd only got secondhand. Something about her just crawled up my ass. Her phoney smile, condescending attitude, petty jealousy, dyed hair, fake nails, and JAP upbringing did little to endear her to me – I hated the way she bounced in the room eager to take us all upstairs to oogle the fresh scars and purple bruises from her implants, a gift from Daddy. I couldn't wait to smash her in the fucking face.

The Long Island Four had lucked out, securing one of the larger rooms in the Chelsea, which was by now, if it hadn't always been, a flea-bitten rat trap whose glorious history of bohemian rhapsody had long since ceased to resonate. The room overlooked 23rd Street, the noise of its traffic filling in the blank silence and greedy anticipation, as speed was chopped out. I didn't do speed, I was edgy enough. I poured myself a glass of Jack Daniels. Smoked some hash that was doing the rounds. Waiting for the show to begin.

Gina was already hopped up on caffeine and diet pills, so she contented herself with a single line. Greedy bitch. I still wanted to smack her. The Long Island Four settled into their usual ritual: snort a line or two, smoke some hash, pour a drink, and speak in code. Over and over again. Sal, acting as lead instigator, clapped his hands three times, saying "Ladies and gentlemen... quiet, please... break out those fucking tits..." Shooting back a slug of Jack and slamming the glass down, he demanded Gina take off her top. A striped number which she slowly unbuttoned, basking in the attention. All eyes on her tits. Still swollen, black and blue around the edges, magenta scars, they were beautiful. A perfect 36C.

A debate ensued between Sal and two members of the Four. Votes taken on preference of real vs fakes. Sal, outnumbered, sided with the silicone. Warren, the one I had my eye on for the past few weeks, insisted on an up-close comparison, suggesting I lend my tits to the conversation. Since I've always considered them one of my finer assets, I had no inhibitions about tweaking them once or twice, coyly exposing first the left, then the right, and finally releasing them from the prison of my clothes. Warren let out a small grunt, walking over and cupping first my tits, then Gina's, hers still sore from surgery. The self-proclaimed expert gently fondled the fleshy mounds checking for ripeness, fullness, contour and sensitivity. Applying tongue and teeth to nipples, he gauged the response. Satisfied with the results, he declared my tits the winner, complaining that Gina's reminded him of a Granny Smith that had failed to blossom. They were stuck forever stitched in place, two hardballs miles from homeplate that might indeed help Gina to score, but had failed to win her this game. In a snit, she screamed "Fuck off you fucking speed freak!!!" and disappeared into the bathroom.

Warren and Sal celebrated her humilation with two more lines, another stick of hash and more Jack Daniels. The other three of the Long Island Four begged off, heading up to Show World to catch one of their girlfriends head-lining a live sex show. Sal insisted they stay, he'd get Gina to put on a show as soon as she was finished in the bathroom. They shrugged it off as old news and split.

Warren invited me over to the fuzzy chair his 6ft 8" frame dominated, insisting I sit on his lap. He was in desperate need of flesh to bounce his speed jitters off of. He grabbed me by both tits, holding on to me like a small pony as he bounced me up and down. Stirring the fiery liquid which was slowly intoxicating me. I was only one more drink from drunk. I asked him to slow it down, let me do the bouncing. I began a slow grind against him, forcing my ass into his crotch, bearing down as I felt him stiffen. Big dick. Small hole. I was getting gooey. He slipped his hands between my legs. Felt the moisture. The heat. Responded by flexing his prick. Sniffing his finger. Sticking it in his mouth. Demanded to taste my pussy. I slip my pants off, straddle the chair. Tease his tongue with pussy. Bury his face in it, pull away. Slam it against him. Pull it away. He catches me between his teeth. Chews on my peach fuzz, the sweet flesh beneath it. Jabs at me with his fleshy tip. I shiver.

Sal, supine on the bed, all the while hissing out directions: "Spread those cheeks, show me some asshole, rim that cunt, suck it... suck it..." until Warren tells him to shut the fuck up. His running commentary a blight on our high. Gina saunters out of the bathroom in her panties and heels. She must have dropped a few more diet pills, you could almost feel her scars crawl. Sal instructs her to come no closer, to turn around, face the wall and bend over, to expose some pink. She smiles demurely mumbling a "Yes Daddy" and does what's expected. Sal and Gina had been screwing each other for years. Hate-fucking.

Sal gets the brilliant idea of dragging me into it. Instructing me to remove my cunt from Warren's face and pick up the coke bottle from the dresser. A filthy leftover from the last tenants. Crusted with dust and dried sugar water. Motions me over to Gina, still obediently bent over, waves me in her direction. Tells me to stick the coke bottle inside her. Stick it in her pussy. Fuck her. Fuck that cunt. I spit on the rim, dribbling a little inside. Gina starts begging, "No Sal, please, not this again..."

"Shut your fucking mouth you scumsucker, open your pussy. Open it, you fucking cunt!"

Gina starts to whine. And wiggle her fucking ass. The bitch thrives on humiliation. She parts her hairy slit, revealing deep purples, browns, grey, pink. Warren cocks his head to improve his view. He's taken his dick out, half erect and moist, resting against his belly. Sal's rubbing his prick against the pillow, slow humping, raised up on one elbow. "FUCK HER YOU FUCK!!!" he bellows, never tiring of playing dictator. I slip the tip of the bottle inside her sloppy hole, moistened by the shouts, the instructions. It swims inside her slick. I pump the bottle slowly inside her, up to the round swell past the neck... The bitch moans, wagging her ass. She actually wants more. I begin to jerk it in, steady pump of glass in cunt. Sal becomes delirious. Shaking his prick, flailing it in circles, squeezing the purple head in both fists, he shouts "Do you fucking know how to fuck???" Leaping off the bed, he grabs the bottle from my hands with a loud plop, as her struggling cunt begs for more fuck. I remember my mother confiding to my aunt about her job in a Coca Cola bottling factory in the late fifties. How they'd supposedly find mice embalmed in bottles, or roaches. She said it was her job to inspect the line to make sure no vermin were visible. How one woman had to be rushed to the doctor, after getting a bottle stuck inside her. That's why coke bottles now have a concave bottoms, so they wouldn't get stuck inside. I was only five when I heard this, but I never forgot it.

Sal was pump-fucking her with the glass cock. Pulling her hair with one hand, pumping with the other, shouting out a string of brutal obscenities. Violent curses. Threatening to jam the bottle up her cunt until she was spitting shards of broken glass. Slapping his cock against her. He spun her around, bottle dangling between her legs, told me to get behind her, keep that cunt full, while she sucked him off.

Gina was shaking, choking on his cock. He had her by both ears, fucking ruthlessly into her face. Suffocating her with his horrible prick. Warren was still blissfully silent, stroking himself off, ready to unload. Group frenzy. Gina sobbing, slobbering, gagging; Sal, bucking quicker still, ready to explode. Me, pumping, slapping her now, punching at her with the bottle. A hideous collective orgasm swept the room. Grunting, groaning, crying, screaming, an audio-nightmare of ungodly proportion. I felt filthied by the hot come which seemed to bathe the room in a ghostly film.

Thirty seconds of silence.

Sal plopped his cock free. I pulled the buried treasure out. Warren scooped a load of sickly white onto the arm of the chair. Sal walked to the window overlooking 23rd Street, grabbed a cigarette and shook his dick at a passing school bus. Gina ran to the bathroom, slamming the door. I took another drink. Lit a roach.

Fifteen minutes pass. We sit there spent, collecting ourselves. Gina re-emerges from the bathroom, showered, wrapped in a towel. Smiling. Sal asks her what the fuck is she oogling. Why is she so fucking happy. What the fuck is wrong with her, why hasn't she left yet. She stammers a "But... Sal..." He tells her to disappear, he can't stand her fucking glee. To get gone. Get out. Get the fuck out. He rushes over, shoving her on her ass, kicking her once for good luck... "What the hell do you want now... you got off, now go!" He rips the towel away from her, snapping it against her thighs. Pulls her up by the hair. Rushes her over to the door, opens it and shoves her out.

Gina pounds on the door, begging to be let back in. Pleading for her clothes, her purse, the ring she left in the bathroom. Sal ignores her, staring out the window picking his ass. Warren, used to years of their bullshit, announces he's taking a bath... would anyone care to join him? The pounding continues, Sal grabs the coke bottle off the floor smashing it into the door. Glass splatters everywhere. Her footsteps trail down the hall. Sal says he's taking a nap. See ya later. I collect my shit to leave. A timid knock on the door. Hotel management, asking for the lady's clothes back. Sal demands "What lady?"

Another timid knock. "Sir, please..."

Sal grabs her clothes and purse, wings them out into the hall, slamming the door. Gina whines about the ring she left in the bathroom. Sal yells for her to fuck off. He'll see her this weekend. She can pick it up then. She kicks the door and storms down the hallway.

Her footsteps fade. The three of us have a drink, Warren pink from soaking, Sal greasier than ever. I decide to split, swearing I'll never see Sal again. Warren walks me to the door, whispering, "I'm gonna fuck you. A good fuck. Next time I see you. Just the two of us. Soon, okay?" He kisses the top of my head. Opens the door, steps aside for me to pass. Bows at the waist. "Bye, beautiful..." He blows me a kiss, slipping behind the door as he eases it shut.

I met up with him a few nights later at Club 82. A stinking basement dive. I dragged him into the ladies' toilet, last stall. We blew a joint and finished our beers. He stood me up on the toilet seat, had me face the wall. Began a glorious finger fuck, penetrating my asshole with long lean fingers, moistened with spittle. Whispered he wanted to smear my shit all over the bathroom walls. Would take my ass until it was so juicy and loose that my bowels would explode, perfuming the room. Wasted, high, horny, he eased another finger in. Then another. Urging me to come, to shit, to erupt. I came screaming, a small trickle of liquid gold expelled from my asshole. He wiped his hands on the stall door drawing a Star of David in chocolate. Licked the last of it from his middle finger. Just as the club's manager walked in, alarmed by our muffled screams. Kicked us out, banning us from returning. Haven't seen him since.

Wore out my welcome with the good doctor. Concocted a new scam. Even less taxing. Took to 6th Ave and 8th Street, equipped with yellow notepad. Claiming to be soliciting funds for cancer research. I'd approach women with small children. Singing a sad song about babies born with incurable diseases, how much a small donation would mean. Our headquarters on 57th Street encouraged by recent breakthroughs, a cure just around the corner. What was needed was more money. The government as usual stingy. It worked every time. A dollar or two added up quickly. I'd retire for the day after milking ten or twenty greenbacks off of guilty liberals. Prey on their heartstrings. Another victimless crime.

It was still easy to skip out on the bill at any number of restaurants. Two people walk in, order, eat. One hits the john, the other disappears. Last man out had the more difficult job of a casual navigation to the exit. An air of indifference is the key to a smooth getaway. Pulled that trick off many times. Until the character I was with got caught. I left first. Propped myself against the designated corner, three blocks away. Fifteen minutes later, my cohort shows up. Two greasy toes sticking out through old holes in tattered socks. Management had confiscated his shoes. Would return them once the bill was paid in full. Cheaper to buy new shoes. Never went back.

Started pilfering from supermarkets. Walk in, wolf down a few quick snacks, stroll to the counter, buy a pack of gum, cigarettes, a banana. Negligible goods. The cheaper the better. Pretend you had a reason to be there. The shitty suprette on 5th Street and 1st Avenue was an easy mark. Thought they were safe, half a block from the precinct. They weren't.

Clothes were always easy to come by. Street vendors selling stolen goods on Astor Place a few bucks a pop. Or a quick jaunt to one of the smaller department stores, dressed in layers to exchange for better shit. Worked fine until they installed surveillance cameras in every dressing room, and even the toilets. Employed undercover grannies to pose as shoppers to eagle-eye the lavatories. Attached those hideous metal tags to every top, trouser, panty.

I had a favourite spot I'd always hit for clothes. A shitty mall in downtown Brooklyn. Must've lifted two grand worth of shit from it. Even when hustling chump change, I needed to look good. Never know who you might run into. Might wanna sweep you away. Might want to suck you off.

I walked in wearing a long leather trench coat. Bound tightly around me. It concealed three complete outfits I was planning to replace. Slipped into a short black dress, lace camisole, patent leather mini-skirt, black velvet jacket and a fifty-two dollar pair of silk panties. The clothes I walked in with were strung up in their place. Headed over to the kid gloves. Should have known better. But I was greedy. The downfall of every criminal.

I could smell him before he put his hand on my shoulder. Small black man, ringer for Sammy Davis Jr. Asking me to come back to his office. Claimed to have been trailing me for months. Gave a run down of everything I had pilfered, a catalogue of infractions I was no doubt guilty of. Said he was calling the police, and if need be, he'd send them over to my house to retrieve every last item I'd pocketed. That's when I cold-cocked him. Dead on the jaw. Massive roundhouse right. Took off running. Watching him splatter into the plate glass window near the exit. I prayed it would break and crucify him with splinters of tinted glass. He toppled.

I must've been high priority. He had radio'd for the cops as soon as he spotted me entering the store. They approached me laughing. They hurried me around the corner and congratulated me for sending Sammy flying. Confided they couldn't stand his self-righteous bullshit. Claimed a nigger in a suit was still a nigger. Asked for my side of the story. Told them it must've been a misunderstanding. Tried some panties on and forgot to pay for them. Asked them if they'd like to look. Hiked my skirt up, a flash of pink twinkling beneath black silk. One of them spotted the fifty-two dollar price tag. Fingered it. Shook his head. Admitted he wouldn't pay for it either. Told me to split. They'd tell Sammy that they lost me in the crowd. Couldn't catch me. Just to spite him. One of the cops slipped me his phone number. Told me to stay out of trouble. Skipped to the subway. Whistling the theme from *Rocky*.

New York City did not corrupt me. I was drawn to it because I had already been corrupted. By the age of six, my sexual horizon was over-stimulated by a father who had no control of his fantasies, natural tendencies or criminal urges. Like father, like daughter. Before my teenage years I had already experimented with mescaline, THC, pot, acid, quaaludes, tuinals, valium and angel dust. I was already an experienced pickpocket, shoplifter, short shift hustler. New York was a giant candy store, meat market, insane asylum, performance stage. Surrounded by five million other junkies, addicts, alcoholics, rip-off artists, dreamers, schemers and unsuspecting marks, New York afforded me the luxury of anonymity. The devil's playground.

Shitty stoop outside some crappy club in Lower Manhattan. Not stoned enough. Two bucks and a token in my pocket. Lipstick and keys. Still squatting with the hippies in Chelsea. Looking for a way out. No fucking clue how. A taxi pulls up, dimmed headlights. Jumps the curb and stops a foot or two from my left knee. The driver cocks his head, says "Get in..." Tell him I'm broke. Says he's not looking for money.

I hop in the front seat. Asks if I want to go to Coney

Island. It's 1:30 in the morning. I ask what for. Says he's gotta make a pick-up. I shrug. He lights a joint, slyly passes it over, turns the radio on, singing along with Gene Pitney to *Town Without Pity*. I plant my boots on the dash. Staring into his profile. A cross between Cagney and Chaney. I remember a lousy late night black & white, *Man Of A Thousand Faces...*

So I'm with another strange fuck. This one's got a fetish for evil clowns. Killer clowns. Alcoholic acrobats. One-armed knife throwers. Midgets, trapeze artists, anything to do with the circus. Being a taxi driver is almost like running away to join the circus every night. So he says. Every kind of freak wants to go here, there, anywhere for a short reprieve from the monotonous chaos of their festered apartments.

I'm no different. I'll jump headlong into anyone's car, pry a little into their night, their life, just to forget my own. Just to forge a new identity for a few hours. A short reprieve from my own chaos. My own monotony.

Cagney's on a roll now. Pissed that *The Last Clown* will never be released. A buried film where Jerry Lewis portrays a painted freak who leads the children of Nazi Germany to the ovens. Says he's started a one man drive to petition Lewis not to buckle to Hollywood pressure, to stick to his guns and get it out. We both know it'll never happen. Everyone needs to cling to a dream, no matter how far fetched, no matter how petty or ridiculous. Cagney claims he'll make it to Hollywood one day, meet with the last great clown and convince him. Keep dreaming, Cagney.

We're cruising the main drag of Coney. All the lights are dimmed, except those illuminating a sleazy old man's bar stuck on the ground floor of the massive, tattered subway station. I already know it's our destination. We pull up to a deserted taxi stand and park. Cagney tells me to wait inside, he'll be back in ten minutes. Incredulous, I ask him if he's joking. He tells me if I get sick of waiting to take the train back to the city. He flips a token into my lap. I call him a fucking asshole and slam the door. He pulls off. I take a chance and enter the bar. Filthy white lights, much too bright for this wasteland of aging dreamers. All so fucking drunk they don't even notice me. Even the bartender's soused. The place stinks of spilled beer, vomit, piss and rot. I pretend to study the jukebox. A horrible selection of Merle Haggard, Patsy Cline, George Jones. *Stand By Your Man* comes on. A toothless grandpa sidles up to me. So sloshed he can barely focus. His sixth sense tells him I'm female. That's all he needs to know. Asks me politely, shyly, pathetically, if I'd like to dance. Out of sheer perversity I agree. He places a sweaty hirsute hand on my hip. I lightly touch his shoulder. Moist with toxic run-off. He quietly sings along, silent tears drenching his dirty face, slicing through the deep crevices, hollowed pocks which litter his cheeks. I pretend he's Bukowski. Not a big stretch. For all I know, he too, has copious volumes of sad old man musing stuck in a browning folder up at the transient hotel he probably calls home across the street near Nathan's Hot Dogs. He smells of years of bad food, booze and self-satisfied sex. I take a twisted pity upon him. Realize it's just one bad turn too many that separates him from me. One rent check too short. One lay-off too soon. One too many broken hearts. And too much fucking booze. I almost want to walk him home. Invite myself in. Clean his battered old man's body. Cut his hair, give him a shave. A manicure. Cook him breakfast. Massage his blistered feet, which reek through his holey shoes. The song ends. I excuse myself, shaking off my demented fantasy, walk into the ladies' room. A sobering experience which disperses the last remnant of my Mother Teresa dreamscape. The single stall is smeared with dried vomit and shit. I decide to piss in the small wastepaper basket overflowing with dirty brown paper towels. Not realizing it's made of mesh. As I piss, a thick trickle ebbs through the weave, flowing toward the entrance. Not that anyone in this dump would notice. I dry myself with the last paper towel, deciding I need to get the hell out of this tortured purgatory where old men sit in out till Judgement Day. Death is always too long in the making. Death can never be hurried. Cold and cruel, Death smugly waits for the body to poison itself beyond repair. Its final spasm will not bring relief, merely erasure.

The hippies finally laid down the law. Wanted me out in three days. Said I was taking up valuable real estate. Yeah, right, the cramped cubicle above John and Yoko's was prime accommodation for a midget with no sense of smell. Of course I'd never paid them the thirty dollars a month they attempted to weasel out of me. But that wasn't the real issue.

Word got out that I was chasing someone around the loft, threatening them with a pair of lawn shears. An insane exaggeration. I had invited Cagney over. The taxi driver who dumped me in Coney. I ran into him outside a night club. Invited him over to smoke a joint. He had no idea I carried a grudge. Of course he probably never rode the F Train from the last exit in Brooklyn to 23rd Street at two in the fucking morning. Never had to fend off a small army of teenage black boys looking to gang rape some white chick stranded on a subway platform in the middle of the night. I got Cagney good and stoned. Brought him up to my bunk. Slipped a small pair of stainless steel scissors out from under my pillow. Snipped off a lock of his hair. He wigged, falling down the rickety ladder that led up to the loft. I scurried down the steps, chasing after him. Laughing like a madwoman while he shrieked like a little girl. He thought I was trying to slash his throat. I might have, if there were any place to dump the body.

He found the front door, bolting out of it yelping murder. Which fucked up John and Yoko's heroin-induced high. That was the final straw. Interrupting their dreamstate. The next day they asked me to leave. I said I'd try to be out by Monday.

I lied.

I headed downtown. At the time South of Canal was a no man's land. Now it's overrun with shitty high-priced restaurants, lofts with a river view and million dollar price tags. Back then, there were a handful of low-rent artists who paid next to nothing to inhabit crumbling buildings in a neighbourhood turned ghost town after dark. It seemed a suitable location to start looking. I'd met a few musicians who operated a bare bones rehearsal studio a few blocks from the Hudson River. I decided to snoop around, see what I could scrounge.

The building next to theirs sat vacant. Four storey pre-war commercial space. Large storefront windows propped up on the sidewalk. Ten feet tall. I scratched a small patch in the muddy glass. The insides a cobwebbed wonderland. Probably empty for years. In the second storey a faded sign with phone number and address. Decided to scrimp on the quarter. The landlord was only a few blocks away.

He was a wheezing over-weight non-practising Jew on his way home to the Island for the weekend. Caught him as he was locking up. I pitched a plea. Told him I'd seen the sign, cooed that I might be able to clean the place up, play building manager. Help him to get the building back on its feet. Maybe even have applications on hand.

A potential client might be made to feel more comfortable if a floor or two were already occupied. Business attracts business. My presence would definitely stir up interest. I could take it over on a trial basis, no lease needed, just see if we could turn the building around. Obviously, for years the space had accumulated dust, not rent. Maybe I could help him turn it around. It would benefit us both. He bought it.

I convinced him to waive the rent. He told me to come back Monday and pick up the keys. And bring a flashlight – the electricity had been turned off since the Kennedy assassination.

The four massive floors were gloriously stripped of everything except the columns that supported them. The third floor was edged in an iron balcony lending it the air of a Vaudevillian strip joint. Huge holes were rusted in the spiral staircases leading up to the gangplanks.

Low-lying puffs of dust sparkled with the soft light that leaked in through pinpricks dotting the roof. The second floor was devoid of any character, a huge blank space once used as store room. The ground floor, which I took as my own, consisted of two massive rooms, fronted by immense store windows. I would construct bizarre set designs in them from junk scavenged from the trash, discarded mannequins, dead flowers, old shoes. The odd passer-by would occasionally wander in, wondering if it was a club, a shop or a brothel.

The basement was the real gem. It held an ancient printing press last used during the Depression. Parts were scattered everywhere, letters spelling out strange haikus on the floor. Old newspapers piled high in every corner, hibernating under inches of dust, dirt, plaster. You could lose yourself for hours, faking headlines on the floor, or in a solitary game of Scrabble. Toward the back of the basement, a small arched door was rotting off its hinges. My flashlight illuminated catacombs extending under the sidewalk fifteen or so feet. Dark dingy tombs only five feet high, lined with damp brick dripping dirty water from rusted pipes. I flashbacked to the Inquisition. Women dressed in tattered burlap, bruised and bleeding, imprisoned on charges of heresy, kept chained and starved, beaten and tortured. Turned into saints for what they didn't believe in. Their leg irons long since rusted away. Mournful screams muffled by the hands of time whose bony fingers had scratched secrets into the dirt floor. It was magical.

At least I was out of 24th Street. The hippies had started to grate. Uptight for dopeheads. They turned green when informed I had my own building. All to myself. Buttered up the musos next door, who were generous enough to let me shower there occasionally. Hadn't been running water in my building for at least a decade. I worked out a deal, ten bucks a month to run a line of electricity down the stairs and into my space. Two sixty watt bulbs hung naked in the centre of the room. I knew I'd only be able to hold out there till winter. But I wasn't thinking that far ahead.

I was thinking about picking up young boys, bringing them back to spend the night, kicking them out in the morning. Becoming a den mother to a herd of fourteen and fifteen-year-old near virgins whose chastity would be forever soiled, spoiled as I sucked up little pieces of their soul in exchange for their first real fuck. Supped on their energy like an insatiable bloodsucker whose belly would never fill. Forever assuring me a bookmark in their history as they became a footnote in mine.

Remember one hot Sunday morning throwing a

farewell fuck to a lucky fourteen-year-old on the sidewalk outside the storefront, while from the other side his two sidekicks jerked off. My knees were scrapped for weeks.

I was pulling the day shift at the Wild West Saloon, a cheesy go-go bar in midtown Manhattan. Cocktail waitressing to make ends meet. Still wasn't paying any rent, but I had to eat. The dancers were an exotic crew of college students, single mothers, substitute teachers, junkies, ex-junkies and just about every other type of female who couldn't stand the typical 9–5. Some dabbled in various forms of adult entertainment, others were lifers. I was just passing through, working every scam I could think of.

Most of the women only lasted a few days or a couple of weeks. I'd pop in for a few shifts when I was completely tapped. There were any number of better places a few blocks away. But they'd I.D. you. And I wasn't yet eighteen. I had a few 'regulars' who'd pay good money for two minute hand-jobs under the sticky tables. Made it tolerable. I put up with the lewd comments and occasional slaps on the ass from the management out of pity laced with disgust.

I had a crush on the barmaid, Judy, a hardcore Irish Butch. We'd turn the odd trick together, servicing obscenely obese men. We'd both sit on top, one mounting, the other shoving a juicy ass on the john's face. We'd make out with each other, biting each other's tongue to suppress the laughter.

It was a slow mid-week day. I always pulled the afternoon shifts. Although they weren't as busy as the evenings, I needed my nights free. One of the dancers came in selling tabs of acid for three bucks a pop. I downed two hits. Waited for the rush. By six I still hadn't come on. Thought I'd been duped.

I went into the bathroom to smoke a joint with Evie, a small Puerto Rican dancer riddled with stretch marks from shitting out two kids. She invited me over to her place for dinner and drinks. To smoke a couple of joints, good Jamaican shit. Still not tripping, I decided to accept.

We took a taxi up to Queens, feeling good after the joint. She told me the kids would be in bed, dinner in the oven, her husband had cooked up a Cuban feast of Yucca, salt cod, beans and rice. It was the first I had heard she had a husband. I just assumed that like most of the dancers she was either single, separated or divorced. That put a new spin on things.

Her apartment was on the top floor of an old Victorian under reconstruction. You could smell the Latino aromas of pork fat and fried bananas before we left the taxi. The sexy strains of Salsa music drifted down the stairs, a welcome relief after six hours of Patsy Cline's *Crazy* and Gloria Gaynor's *I Will Survive*... the stable irritants of the tittie bar.

Her husband, Castro's third cousin, greeted us at the door with a warm smile and too-tight bear hug. Urging us in, telling us to sit down, take our shoes off, we must be exhausted. Go lay down if we wanted, dinner would be ready in twenty minutes. He handed us a bottle of cheap Spanish wine and a fat joint.

Evie led me by the hand on a guided tour littered with cheap red satin love seats, worn Mexican rugs, children's toys scattered in corners, a Cuban flag draped proudly as a curtain across the huge four-poster bed, probably a family heirloom. She suggested we lay down, put our feet up. Allow the greasy edge of the Wild West to wear off. Hustling drinks in four-inch pumps for six hours straight can make you brain-dead. A little catnap to recuperate.

The soft bed, her soothing voice and the pot began to kick in. I began to doze off almost as soon as my head hit the pillow. Bad dreams. Troubled nightmares. The acid was kicking in, in my sleep. Visions of mad butchers stringing up young girls on meat hooks. Filleting their labias with surgical instruments. Slicing off pieces of thin, bloody flesh. Female castration. Their agonizing screams shook me from my nightmare. I woke up to one of Evie's kids crying, held in the huge Cuban's hairy paw. Who stood at the foot of the bed. Watching Evie stuff her crotch in my face. I woke up tripping. Her cunt a swell before my eyes. The lips bleeding as she twisted them. Purple, pinks, blood red, wounded. A giant insect twitching its multiple folds inches from my face. I started to lose it. Freaked out. Began screaming at her husband, the mad butcher. Demanding to know what he had done... what he planned on doing to me. Why had he taken my clothes off... where were they? Threatening to call the police if he didn't immediately call me a cab. I had to get out of there. They began screaming at each other in Spanglish, he questioning why she had brought this psycho over, she screaming he shouldn't have been watching. And both babies crying hysterically.

I grabbed my clothes and ran to the bathroom, slipped on a child's toy and cracked my head on the mirror. They thought I was in there destroying the place. I was so fucking high I couldn't see straight. Walls bleeding into the floor, colours folding. Scrambled into my clothes. Stumbled out the door. Beeline to the exit. Forgot the first floor was under construction. Scaffolds, ladders, drop cloths, a haunting maze difficult to navigate. I thought I'd never find the front door. I could hear the taxi honking and followed the sound. Shot into the back seat. "Manhattan, downtown, anywhere..." I could still hear the screaming babies. Kept repeating, "Calm down, you're just high."

I could feel my pupils painfully expanding. Turning my vision fisheye. The taxi now a warm womb bathed in pale molasses, flooded with ochre, amber, burnt sienna, gold. The street lights loomed like melting moons. Stoplights burned new planets. I was relieved to watch the Cuban nightmare fade in the distance.

Pleasantly whacked, I no longer wanted to go home. Got dropped off at 12th Street and 3rd Avenue. Called James, a friend who had just moved into the city from Brooklyn, sub-letting a beautiful apartment. Empty other than a couch and two chairs. A loft bed in the back. He greeted me with a slippery grin, one side of his face melting in upon itself. Wearing a classic fifties smoking jacket, open to the waist, black Levi's and leather moccasins. Himself, high on acid.

At 6ft 7" he towered over me, his deep baritone suddenly turning soprano laugh. We'd been fucking each other every couple of weeks for a few months. Usually while tripping. Between other fucks. His bi-sexual tendencies fascinated me, and he'd often share hilarious details insisting on a confidentiality that was difficult to maintain. It was hard not to divulge juicy tidbits like him having to visit the Emergency Room to have inanimate objects removed from his rectum. Deodorant bottles, shampoo caps, plastic toys.

James asked if I'd care to join him in a drink. Invited me to get comfortable on the couch, he'd be right in to serve me. He floated into the kitchen, returning with a five-pound jar of honey. Giggling as he bent over me, pouring forth enough of the liquid coagulant to almost drown me. It boiled out over my lips, a living breathing organism which engulfed my throat, my hair. I felt as if my entire body would be coated in a sticky mummification ritual performed by this snickering Lurch.

Scolding me as if I were a naughty child who had soiled her party dress, he insisted upon cleaning me up immediately. He gently pried open my sticky lips, scooping up fingerfuls of gooey sugar water mingled with spit. He sucked his index finger seductively, darting his tongue between his hand's fleshy web. Kneeling beside me, his flat, fat tongue and womanly lips lapped at my neck, his intoxicating mouth painting strange hieroglyphs toward my breasts. He would glue his lips to small pieces of my flesh, dissolving the thick honey into our skins. Drawing arcane symbols with tongue and teeth. Suckling, then chewing on my tight little nipples until I thought I'd left my body. A large, slow animal feasting on fresh meat.

It was close to midnight when the third rush hit. Twelve hours after I had ingested the shit. Still flying. We had showered together like a lop-sided brother and sister, conspiring on the mischief to follow. We decided to stage an orgy. Playing the centrepieces. Dressed in towels as saris and turbans, we began phoning everyone we knew. Whether we had sexed them already or not. Inviting them to come over and fuck us. After the first initial rejections, we became even bolder, randomly dialling numbers like a lottery. Our hysteria and manic tone ensured that the invitations would remain unheeded.

Slightly disappointment, we decided to to fuck each other, until a bicycle left in an empty closet caught our attention. It struck us as the most ridiculous instrument we'd ever seen. Armed with dull butter knives, we began to dismantle it. Removing the tires, rims, spokes from the rims, the seat, the handlebars. Giggling like idiots, howling with laughter, we began to throw pieces out the window into the concrete courtyard three storeys below. The hideous clamour chimed to us like church bells at a family picnic. We'd spasm with laughter every time another useless piece was launched overboard, shouting out punchlines from juvenile poetry.

We passed out at four, after a couple hours of light diddling. High, exhausted, spent from laughing so much, we finally collapsed. I woke a few hours later greeted by three cops in riot gear. Chatting over steaming cups of coffee, admiring my nudity. I had no idea how long they had been standing there. Was surprised they hadn't taken liberties with my inebriate form. Or maybe they had and I was too fucked up to notice. I asked them if they had a coffee for me. They laughed insisting they had more than coffee... I bantered if they were looking for recruits, they had landed on the wrong planet. I was terminally unemployable. And what the hell were they doing here anyway. They claimed they were sent to investigate a "disturbance". They got the call six hours before.

Typical.

I had no idea where my host had gone. Maybe work. He was publishing fraudulent biographies and selling them to Europe. He'd pick on someone he truly hated, like Michael Douglas or Motley Crüe, and pen two hundred page bio's based on the worst bullshit he could make up. As if anything could be possibly worse than how truly awful they really were. Anyway I needed to get dressed, needed fresh air to stave off the migraine licking at my frontal lobes. I informed the officers if there was nothing more I could do for them, to please leave. The fat bald Italian whispered "Ohh... there's plenty you could do...," squeezing his nightstick in both hands. The fat tip of a coffee-stained tongue darting obscenely across his blistered lower lip. A gruesome vision which I struggled to shake off.

Two dozen lines were laid out on the musty dresser. A pocket-sized transistor radio belted out classic R&B through the static. I was pulling a trick with Judy, the barmaid from the shithole I occasionally worked at. She had set up the gig at a lousy midtown low-rent hotel within walking distance from the bar she still tended. She was on a lunch break. Servicing two black dealers from the Midwest, who'd head into town every few months to pick up a shipment, check the shit out, blow off a couple of grams, a grand or two and head back to Detroit.

She was well into blowing the ringleader by the time I'd arrived. My 'date' greeted me at the door immaculately dressed in deep purple polyester pant suit complete with wide-brimmed hat, pinkie rings and gold canine tooth. He bowed at the waist and ushered me in. Leading me over to the dresser, he supplied me with a short glass straw. Inviting me to indulge. Loosen up. Get comfortable. Checking out my round ass as I bent over to sup. Judy's mouth full of cock, took it all in, letting out a small chortle. Tricking with her was playtime. She had a great attitude about sex, only fucking men for money. Had to support her seven-year-old son. Put her girlfriend through law school. Fast sex for hard cash helped.

I sniff up two or three lines under my 'date' Leon's urging, who's by now himself so high, he's sprawled out on the bed, rubbing a huge prick through rough polyester. The shit kicks into my skull like a wayward rocket ricocheting around inside my head. "Come suck on your Big Daddy you sweet white ho..."

I do what I'm told, slipping a Trojan over his rainbow-coloured cock. I position myself over him, off to one side affording him the faint waft of hot pussy. He slips his thumb inside succulent wet walls of flesh, pulls it out sucking on it like a toddler. Mumbling a non-stop flurry of "oohhh baby's" and "that's it mama's". I roll my eyes and continue to blow him. Locking eyes with Judy, who's adopted the same position, ass in the air toward the john's face, who like my trick is busy babbling while anointing his fat black lips with her sluice. She begins to mimic my every movement. We roll our eyes in unison. Stick out our tongues. Make obscene hand gestures. Reminiscent of a Harpo Marx-Lucille Ball mirror trick from *I Love Lucy* re-run on late night TV. We both crack up, laughing hysterically, simultaneously tumbling off the queen-size bed almost knocking each other out. The johns think we've lost our minds.

Erections flag. Time to suck up a few more lines. Take this shit to another level. Judy and I always ready to milk it out. We'd charge by half-hour increments. Spend most of the time goofing off, playing with each other, talking the tricks in circles, giving them massages, anything to keep the actual time spent fucking and sucking to a quick burst. That was all most of the johns needed. More than what most of them deserved. Generous bitches, weren't we?

But these two brothers knew what they wanted. Paid to get it. As soon as a dozen more lines were sucked up, they were hard again. Hungry for pussy. White pussy. Pink pussy. Good pussy. Pussy that would bang up and down, pounding long lean pricks in a monotonous hammering, an endless battering. Pussy that knew how to work for that dollar. Would work for that dollar until both cock and cunt were too raw to touch, too raw to fuck, too fucking raw to even look at any more. And so we pounded. We sat on top of them, banging into them like battering rams. We spun around on their pricks, our backs to them, so we could watch each other. Judy pumped like a cheetah, her short red hair, pale skin sprinkled with freckles, iridescent green eyes, long legs, rode that bastard like a caged animal returned to the wild, slaughtering her first kill. She was yelling at her trick to come. To "shoot that fucking come inside that tight white pussy..." That was it. He came inside her howling like a wounded puppy. I was still grinding away, just about ready to lose my high, when Judy, soaked in musky perfume, came over to squeeze my tits with wet fingers trailing the intoxicating aroma of her hot sex. Pulling on my nipples, squeezing and twisting. Spanking my swollen little clit. Whispering in my ear "You like this too much, you horny little slut." I came all over her fingers, spraying hot juice all over the trick's cock, balls, down the crack of his ass. Judy spit on her middle finger and stuck it straight up his black asshole. A few quick pokes and he was ready to squirt. I banged myself against him bruising my pelvic bone with every thrust. The shit finally came screaming a string of ridiculous obscenities which caused us both to giggle. We politely excused ourselves, collected the cash from the dresser, took a quick shower and split. French kissing as we hailed two cabs.

The first few years spent in New York were a blur of alcohol, sex and drugs. I had moved from crash pad to squat to storefront to a series of cheap apartments in tenements. Chelsea, Tribeca, East 2nd, 3rd and 4th Streets, Delancey, East 12th in three different apartments in the same building, Spanish Harlem, Murray Hill, Brooklyn. Running up overdue bills. Disappearing in the middle of the night, usually on a whim, invited to sleep on somebody's couch, take over their spare room, or share their bed. It was easy to bum around. Occupancy rates were down, rent control was still in effect, people were more generous. Less suspicious.

There were any number of ways to avoid having to actually hold down a job. I knew every single one of them. When I was truly desperate, I'd put a few days in at tittie bars, go-go clubs, strip joints. I enjoyed hustling for drinks, the false promises, leading men on, taunting, weaseling money off of lonely degenerates. I hated the long hours, sleazy management, and trips to Jersey when the gigs ran out in Manhattan. Loved the power pussy had. The way men were drawn to its mysteries, as if prospecting for gold in foreign territory. Sweet evil flower, instrument of torture and ecstasy. Delicate blossom, root of deception. Buried deep in its fleshy folds, so very many ancient secrets, a magic which has confounded men since it was banished from the Garden, full of Voodoo whose spell turns men into monsters.

Decided it was time to cut to the chase, eliminate the middle man. Cultivated a few 'regulars' from the bars who could afford to pay me by the hour what I'd usually pull in a day or two. My overhead was incredibly low, since I rarely paid rent, but I still needed cash. Tricking could accumulate the most money while exerting the least effort. I thought it was an invaluable service, filling a small pocket of a lonely man's life with momentary joy. Flooding the dark night of their psyche with my light, my youth. My pussy a place where they came to worship, which offered up relief from a petty existence frustrated by work, wife, kids, responsibility.

Tricking, to me, was the ultimate freedom. A blank screen onto which you could project any image you want. A relapse from reality. A place where I could excommunicate my self from myself. I would dissolve into a thinly veiled disguise replete with alias, game plan, M.O., fake I.D. I took a strange pity on the men I serviced. Had more respect for them than most of my other relationships. Everything was on the level: you sell them a fantasy for thirty minutes or an hour. They get what they pay for. You get what you need. Money. And then they leave. No bullshitting. No babysitting. No hand-holding. Most men were too needy. Desperate. Dependent. Little boys, never able to murder that little girl inside of them. Always begging for love, compassion. Constant attention. Confirmation of their manhood. Sexual recognition. Phallic worship. Just like a john, only they resented paying for it. But they still get milked. One way or another.

Through some twisted miracle I was able to avoid syphilis, gonorrhoea, herpes simplex I & II, genital warts and AIDS. I was either blessed, or I belonged to the minuscule percentage of the genetic population which is truly immune to such unfortunate viral infections.

Of course I suffered monthly. Excruciating blasts of dull pain as inner organs swelled and ebbed blood. Plagued by an all-consuming throb that rendered me useless, impotent, confined to the menstrual hut, where I was overcome by blood visions of the devil dancing on my ovaries.

Every twenty-one days – yes, since every aspect of my life was accelerated, the monthly monster came every three weeks – I was plunged gut-first into a fevered dervish, where hormonal fluctuation conspired to spin me into hallucinatory torpitude. Confined to bed, I would drift in and out of consciousness. Fantastical dreamscapes only a body flushed with pain could produce. Leftover religious delusions wormed into the spaces between nod and R.E.M. A parade of tortured saints, their horrifying lives of torment and rapture played out in a terrifying technicolour. Ruby, maroon, burgundy, emerald, viridian, magenta, violet... every shade of blue. Their glowing robes tattered, shredded, stained by seeping sores. Wounds inflicted, tolerated, embraced as testaments to their faith, their love, their agony. Moments of their lives rolled into a mini-drama in my dreams. Chased, mocked, hounded, surrounded by the evil grins and grimaces of ghoulish apparitions, the sainted ghosts of my vision were the willing victims of a sordid morality play. Punchline prayers never decreed a winner in the age old Saint vs Sinner controversy. And hell... I'm no angel. I've always sided with the bad guys.

Late night afterhours club. Not yet sunrise. Early morning feeding frenzy. Looking to nourish the life's blood. Feels like a bust, when the corner illuminates a Latin Lothario playing solitaire. We're sitting diagonally across from each other, I'm crossing and uncrossing my legs, flashing black panties as he licks his lips. The gauntlet of drunken punters obscures our view. It ups the ante of our little game. He cocks his head back, bites his lower lip, rests his left hand on his inner thigh. I dead-eye him as I open my legs, slowly inching closer to the edge of the crushed velvet couch. Throw my head back a little. Drop my eyes from his mouth to crotch and back again. Show him the candy-coloured tongue dancing in my mouth. Trail him with my eyes, as I get up and leave the room. Of course he follows.

I step into sky blue pink puking up another day. Light a cigarette, drag deep. He's standing beside me. "Come home with me..."

I close my eyes, whisper "Why?"

"So I can blow coke up your ass and fuck you breathless..."

"Get a cab..."

We slip into the dingy backseat of the aging yellow

beast. It stinks of boozy sweat, cigarettes and chewing gum. A real aphrodisiac. I balk when my temporary distraction directs the driver to Queens. The last time, the only time, I went to Queens, I left with hallucinations of butchery and mutilation. This time however, I was sober, not tripping on blotter, stoned on pot or drunk. Not high. Not yet...

The ride seems quick, the skyline of Manhattan disappearing into sunrise. And he's got my shoes off, sucking on one dainty foot, while grinding the other into his full crotch. I stare out the window, blasé, not yet high, not yet turned on. He slips my shoes back on, after deeply inhaling their leathery perfume, and pays the fare, escorting me into a lush duplex. The entire apartment is done in soft creams, off whites, ochres. Huge bay windows showcase the necropolis we just departed. We still haven't really spoken to each other. There's no reason to. Easy Latin listening swells gently around the room. He disappears into the kitchen to fix drinks, a light champagne punch. Returns with an opal tray set with delicate crystal glasses, a cocktail shaker, and small mirrored box full of finely ground cocaine. He offers a silent toast and the twinkle returns to my eyes. Perhaps just a small illumination from the mirrored box of sexual miracles he just set down and opened. He produces a petite silver coke spoon, dips it in the box, holds my chin, devouring me with his dark eyes, and places it under my left nostril. I close my eyes and sup. He repeats the ritual two or three times, never taking his eyes off my face. Infatuated with the expansion in my pupils as the blue of my eyes are erased by black. Then he helps himself. Three quick snorts up each nostril. Rubs a little on my lips. Starts to lick them. To bite them. Corners my lower lip between his canines. Draws a small ruby of blood. I can feel his heart race. Mine too. He cups my face, whispers in my ear, "Turn over, give me your ass..." I prop myself on the

---

Lydia Lunch

back of the soft leather, allowing him to slowly lift my skirt, slowly pull aside my panties. He leaves me there for a moment. Steps across the room, admiring his game. Returns with a small silver straw. Packs it with the white devil. Does as promised back at the club. Blows it up my ass.

Six long lines of coke later and the skin sings. Memory collapses. Time disappears. Thought is replaced with sensation. Every molecule expanding outward teleported into a parallel dimension. Breath hits pockets of pure oxygen, every pore responds, enhanced by a rush of electricity.

Entranced, slow gyrations replace apathy. I can no longer sit still. Every muscle begins to deep grind. He backs up a few feet, watching me squirm. "What do you want me to do, you horny little bitch... Fuck you??? Not yet..." He's backlit in the centre of the spacious cream womb we inhabit. I can't remember his face as he stands three feet away from me, features blurred as the sun splays behind him. I'm so high I astral project. I'm watching us from somewhere beyond the ceiling. Watching him ball up his fist and strike his prick a few times. Like a drunken boxer punishing himself with slow, steady, deadly blows. I see myself, still sprawled out over the creamy couch, pulling my panties further to the side, exposing pink. We're both hypnotized. A manic edge starts to swell, swallowing us. I leave the couch and crawl on all fours, lapping at his thick fists. He continues to pound himself, slow, steady, deadly. He removes his belt, methodically cracking my ass once or twice. Asks me if I like it. I nod my head, lowering it as I raise my ass. Every time he knuckles his cock, he beats my crack, causing my pussy to quiver. I moan like a happy animal.

I return to my body. Rabid. Unleash his prick. Lick. Suck. Swallow it. Deep throat him and hold it there.

Suffocating myself with musky cock. Refuse to relinquish even an inch of prick until I almost pass out. Come up for air hungry, greedy. He encircles himself in a tight fist. Beats the head against my lips, not allowing me to suck or swallow. Slapping roughly his thick, engorged meat against cheeks, allows it to rest at my nursing mouth. I suckle the tip.

He forms a noose with his belt. Slips it around my neck, sweetly pulling my hair free. Drags me crawling behind him like his favourite pet. Walks me into the kitchen. Snowy white tiles, immaculate gleam. Lifts me up unto the spotless counter which occupies centre stage. Sits me facing him. Belt loosely dangling. Reaches under the counter for an industrial-sized box of thick plastic wrap. Begins to encase my breasts, upper torso tightly. Wrapping and rewrapping until I'm mummified in clinging film. Cuts it off with a small sharp boning knife. Licks the edge of wrap. Seals me tight. Mechanically cuts off a large sheet. Wraps it around my face, sealing in my breath. I feel like a blow-up doll ready to burst. He plants his mouth over my nose and mouth, sucking out the last of my breath. Holds his mouth over mine seconds too long. He senses my asphyxia. Lowers himself to my crotch. Sucks, bites, swallows until I come quickly, flooding his face and neck with juice. He raises up, slowly cutting a small hole between my lips. Holding the sharp blade inside my mouth until I lick and suck. He drags it out, carefully slicing a tiny paper cut on my lower lip, whose blood he's already tasted. He drinks again. A single drop. Tears the plastic from my face. I slump, sucking for air.

He pulls me to him, embracing me like a small child. Strokes my face, my hair. Pushes it from my lowered eyes. Draws them up to him. Locks in. Circles my throat with one hand. Firmly. "Come..." He slides me off the counter, leading me by the scruff of the neck back into the living room. Walks me to the couch, applies pressure, forcing me to kneel in front of him. Sticks his first two fingers in the mirrored box. Plants the thick white tips deeply up my nose, into my mouth, down my throat, back up my nose. Holds. Removes and savours.

I forget where I am, who I am. But know why I'm there. I turn away from him, exposing myself. Peeling damp panties over my obscene roundness. Sticking my sex straight up in the air, an overheated cougar stalking rough prey. He slinks over to me, lifting me with fat fingers coaxed into juicy cavities. Tight little holes whose greedy mouths make slurpy sounds around his digits. "You can't stand it any more, can you... you need my fuck, don't you. Don't you???" he taunts.

I whisper "Yes, you fuck..."

He slams himself inside me. Holds me pierced on his prick. One hand scooping my throat, bending my head back, off to one side, forcing me to watch his cool evaporate. Replaced with rage, frenzied fuckface. Thrashing his head from side to side banging slim hips into round ass. Relentless delivery. Banging us both into oblivion. Throttling me with the force of his manic hammering. Every few minutes rearranging positions. From behind, on top, sideways, against the wall, straddling, bent over, on his lap, upside down, searching frantically for the smoothest, deepest route in. He puts me back on top of him, cupping my ass in magic fingers which never cease to kneed, pull, pinch, twist. Pulling me open, spreading me apart, deep bounces up and down for what seems like hours until we collapse. Both too exhausted and numb to even come. We pull apart, drenched, drained, brain dead. "Let's go to sleep..." he purrs. I lie and say I'll be right in, I'd like to shower. He tells me to help myself. Disappears into the plush bedroom. I slip into the shower, its cool pulsating jets of liquid balm soothing the mauled little animal. Coming down and well spent I get dressed. Decide to leave after helping myself to a makeshift bindle. Sorry I'll never see him again. I just couldn't. Bad for my health. That cocaine.

Momentary satisfaction. Quick fix. Forever on the prowl. Obsessed with their dicks just long enough to wash the taste out of my mouth. Then I wanted more. Needed more. Needed to possess them. Tiny nuggets of their souls. Glut on it. Gag on it. Puke it out. Feed again.

Basement bathrooms in shitty Bowery bars. Favourite stomping ground. Alcohol lubricates the libido. Wears down their resistance. Right, like they had any resistance. Order a double vodka. Scan the room. Pick a target. Zero in. Lead them by their dicks downstairs. Shove them into a cubicle. Lock the door. Bark out orders. Make them pull on themselves while sucking me off. Force them to kneel. Grovel. Prove how filthy they really are. Suck my ass. Drink my piss. Fuck them while squatting over the scummy toilet. Banging myself off. Using their t-shirts to sop up the runny juice. A perfume stained with sweaty sex. The lingering afterglow of a hot five-minute fuck. Their only reminder of me as I disappear up the stairs, out of the bar, back on the street. Temporary fix for an unscratchable itch.

Stumbled into the club stoned on Xanax. He was propped against the bar, one arm draped around his girlfriend's shoulder. I cut right in. No bullshitting. Whispered in his ear to meet me on the third floor in two minutes. Smiled at her as I climbed the stairs. Legs made liquid by the pills. Hot flush which moistened panties. Dry mouth. Twitching. Snatched a drink from some chippy who was making her way to the exit. Swallowed it down, handed her back the empty glass. Asked for a refill. She almost started crying. I spat in the glass. Floated upstairs. He was right behind me.

Damaged lyricist, lead singer and ringleader of the Blank Generation. I had screwed him once before. Needed another taste. Pulled him against me. Deep-throating him with my tongue. Rubbing plump titties across his. Thick grind. Damp crotch.

Tiny little cubby. Groping each other behind a broken door in the corner. Grabbing handfuls of juicy prick, rubbing the wet tip, smearing him all over himself. A heady musk inflames lust. Thrust myself against him. Stuff him inside. Ride his fleshy prick until I come spraying all over his cock, his balls, the front of his jeans. Pull him out. Jerk him off. Make him come. Autographing the wall, the door, his t-shirt. Which I wipe my pussy on. Smiling.

Imagining the look of disgust on his girlfriend's mug when he rejoins her at the bar. The smell of my pussy traced into his collar, his hands, his hair. Scarlet stain on his neck, where I bit and chewed. The argument that was sure to follow. Unnecessary, really. She should be grateful. I took what I wanted, but I gave him right back. Now he'd be able to fuck her twice as long when they went home to make up after their little squabble. If she let him. Didn't matter. He'd still be thinking about me. With or without her.

Needed a bigger hustle. Sick of scratching after scraps. Took up too much time servicing just one john at a time. Had to crank it up another notch. Manipulation elevated to Art

Form. Put it up on the stage. In front of an audience, who like johns, pay by the hour, the half hour, or in this case, every ten minutes. Instead of pleasure, sell them pain. My pain. Their own pain. Regurgitated and spat back at them. A public platform for psychotherapy. Make them pay to be tortured. Assaulted. Abused. The audience as whipping boy, whose sex could and would be used against them.

Obliterate the safety net that separates the spectator from the exhibitionist. The doctor from the patient. Play wet-nurse to nightsickness. Detail every form of madness, hysteria, torture, obsession. An unholy vortex of verbal abuse. A hideous din. Around which forms a cult of negation. The figurehead, a fallen Goddess, whose cruelty and hatred would be embraced. Revered. Reviled. Feared. A classic nihilist's philosophy the only dogma: "That which does not kill me, makes me stronger..."

I throw the phone-book to the floor. Kick it in the corner. Shake my head, crack my neck, check my lipstick. Open the door. Frozen, then slowly drawn down the stairs, up the street, past the subway. A thick lull surrounds. Audio hallucinations, swells of deafness, a pleasant cocoon blots out everything except the daydream I'm drifting on.

He almost runs into me. Sandy-blond Greek. 19. On a ten speed. Jeans, boots, belt. Grabs my hand, begs apology, cup of coffee, five minutes to make up for his blunder. Shitty diner. Offers to take me to Montauk for the weekend. We meet at Grand Central or Port Authority or Penn Station for the 6.20. I lie about my age, my address, my name. I forget his. He rambles on about fate, destiny, he knew this was going to happen, premonition... I smile out the window, nodding slowly. *So did I*, I whisper. My eyes heavy with predation. *So did I.*

Cool wet mist slips in as we exit the train. His innocent joy contagious. I allow it to consume me, envelop me, easy to pretend I'm someone else. Easy to believe that the rain married to his wet mouth against mine will cleanse the horrid stench of the rest of the world from my breath. Easy to believe I'll be able to forget who and what I am, lost in the slip of his tongue as it sweeps my mouth on the small front steps of this rundown motel.

We quickly check in, run to the beach. Heavy fog, light drizzle, deserted landscape. End of the season. Everyone's gone. Sorrowful late night song of a filthy battered gull echoes like land's end. Run to the water praying it swallows and sucks us both under. He drops to his knees, rubbing his wet face against wet thighs. Pulls down my zipper, wiggling tight pants down over my ass, down under my pussy. Whispers into my hair a gentle kiss. A deep breath. I pull him in. Tuck my hand between shirt and neck, beg him to lick, to lick, keep licking. I open myself up to his tongue, stuck rigid against my lips.

Make him shove it in my sticky sweet meat, cleaved apart by my anxious fingers pinching my clit. Forcing the tiny head to explode with blood which I'd love to squirt into his mouth as I come all over his beautiful face.

As my spasms subside, he crawls around behind me, lapping at me on all fours, stuffing his face deep in the crack of my ass. Deep breaths. Drinking in my perfumed sex. He buries himself deeper, teasing, tickling. Running circles with his tongue against the bullseye. Taunting small contractions. Coaxing me to fuck his tongue, to suck his tongue with my ass, pulling me against his probing fleshy spear. His greedy mouth banging and biting me into coming. Again.

He pulls me onto the sand, face to face. Tells me to taste my sweet ass, sticks his tongue out, till it reaches mine. I circle it in my mouth, panting on all fours, hungry bitch. He asks me, begs me, tells me, demands to take my ass. Now. He slips behind me, his juicy prick moist in his hands. Rubs it against me talking filthy in Greek. Translates it for me, "I'm going to fuck you until you pass out... and when you wake up I'll still be fucking you..." He presses himself into me. Slow. Opening my tiny chestnut hole with one hand, guiding himself into me with the other. Whispering for me to breathe deeply, open up, relax, enjoy. His thick cock pulsing inside me. Sneaking its length into me. Smooth. Telling me to suck him in, breathe his cock in. I slow my breath down, work him from the inside. My asshole twitching, jerking. He knows I'm ready and begins a steady pump, smooth hot cock causing delirium. I buck back into him, thrashing my head from side to side, urging him to pound into me, to fuck the shit out of me. Begging him to. He pulls out, gripping himself, and begins tonguing me again. Just enough for me to miss his cock, just enough to hear the words *fuck me, fuck me, fuck me...*

I caught the 5.45A.M. train back to the city. I waited until he passed out, slipped thirty dollars out of his wallet and took off. I didn't 'sleep' with anybody... couldn't stand the thought of waking up groggy to get groped by some strange dick that might have been hot the night before. But daylight casts a different pallor. A pallor I didn't want to witness, didn't want to smell the sleep leeching off. Didn't want to deal with who or what I had done. Wanted to languor in the memory long enough to shower it off. Forget as soon as possible all but the temporary satiation that anonymous sex with a complete stranger could uniquely provide.

Played social worker to the bums on Bowery and Grand. I'd bring them sandwiches, bandages, booze. They were banned from the liquor store on the corner. Ms Diana was a female impersonator in his late forties. Dressed in tattered costumes salvaged from off-Broadway playhouses. Tacky lamé turbans piled two to three feet high, resting on top of rotted blonde wigs. Wandered up to NYC in the early sixties to escape the persecution of a Southern upbringing. Would sing a song for the price of a scrambled egg on buttered roll breakfast. Something by the Supremes, Martha and the Vandellas, The Shangri-Las.

"The Foot" kept to himself. A filthy rag and bone man loaded down with half a dozen hefty bags filled with mouldy clothes. I'd slip him a dollar, a donut, a slice of pizza. He'd nod, fold his hands in prayer and lower his eyes, whispering a silent thankyou. The stench of gangrene a noxious cloud of putrefaction.

"The Nose" kept vigil across the street. His swollen proboscis too sensitive, a rotting tomato dissolved by open sores. Proselytizing to passers-by to liberate themselves of material goods. Give up their apartments, blood money paid to miserly landlords. Quit their jobs. Slave labour. Share their money, clothes, his fellow brethren, the heir apparent. Screaming at all who passed to rise up out of the pit of vipers. Relinquish their greed. Petty ambitions. False gods. Unreasonable hopes. Promising that "THE END WAS NEAR... NEARER THAN YOU THINK..." as he held out an old coffee cup, stirring the pennies, nickels, dimes together. An irritating nursery rhyme which jangled the nerves. Causing shudders.

Eddy the Vet lived in a cardboard box on the corner of Prince. Couldn't figure out how to screw his head back on after his capture in Da Nang. Waking hallucinations the target of vicious tirades. The enemy lurking in red Toyotas, Hondas, hatchbacks. Theorized that taxi drivers were U.S. prisoners of war. Claimed to recognize every cab that passed. Had a story to back it up. Couldn't shut him up once he started talking. Terrible tales trailed up the block, burned into the back of your head.

He boarded at 86th Street. Young Puerto Rican boy, no more than fourteen. Small, thin boned, frail. Massive baby browns lined with sadness. Our eyes devoured each other.

He smiled as my pulse boomeranged. I held my tongue in, wanted to grab his big mouth and swallow. He cocked his hips in my direction. Skinny thing. Smiling, teasing, enjoying the attention. We hit 34th Street. He disappeared. My mouth dropped. Kicking myself. I couldn't believe I'd let him slip away. Usually I'd pounce. Pursue. Persuade. Pull them aside. Take them with me. He slipped out the door before I could say a word.

Two weeks later. Same scene. Heading uptown. I had just moved to Spanish Harlem. He gets on at 34th. I had summoned him. All my dreams about his small hands, hard cock, big mouth were about to pay off. I smiled. He lit up. Grabbed his brother's arm. Quick Spanish. "I told you man,

I told you I'd see her again..." I asked him where he was getting off. 110th. My stop. So close to home. Didn't dig that shit. Liked to keep a bit of distance. Nothing too personal. I only wanted a quick, nasty fuck. Not fucking puppy love.

I went for it anyway.

He lied and said he was sixteen. I lied and said I was twenty-two. It didn't matter. We both knew what we wanted. Liquid dreams quenched. He wanted to follow me home. With his brother. I wasn't in the mood for 'legal' tender. The brother was too old. Not hot. Facial hair.

We made a date to meet in the small park on 103rd. Park, right... two cement bleachers stuck on a sidewalk where the remnants of grass ghosts couldn't even cast a shadow. This I couldn't rush. It'd be over with soon enough. One fuck wonder. Had to evaluate a few things first. Like what he boosted. If he hustled. How many brothers he had. How close he lived. In NYC, a few blocks can mean a world apart.

I was hoping...

Another New York hard luck story. He "used" to move coke for his uncle, a Dominican up on 113th. Handled the small runs. Nothing big time. Didn't touch the shit himself. Yeah, feed me another line, baby... Hated what it did. What it made you do. Saw too many of his brothers take one hit too many. Turned them into freaks. Freak. Just smoke the weed. Feel good. Mellow out. He passed a joint underhand. Smiling. Cheap, dirty Mexican. Didn't matter.

The sun bounced, played tricks on his toffee lips. Got swallowed up in the beautiful chocolate freckles bridging his beautiful nose. I watched his nervous hands dance on his bony knees hiding beneath thin black chinos.

Grabbed his wrists. Led him the six blocks, five flights up to my apartment. Twisted the locks open and closed. Grabbed his face. Licked. Tasting sun, soap, sweet

Spanish cheeks. Tongues colliding. I forced him against the door. Crushed him under my dominant size. Experience. Hips grinding into his. Hard. Slipped my hand in his pants. Squeezing cock, balls, full teenage erection. Sweaty. I pulled him out. Firm clasp. Small gasp from parted lips. Which I sucked down in soul kiss. Lost in his deep wet eyes. Let a thick spittle leave my mouth to grease his prick. Perfect aim. Dribble-soaked dick being squeezed in life/death grip. Twisting the head just enough to almost hurt. Testing. To see what he's made of. I shove him back against the door. Walk away.

Of course he follows. Stops at the foot of the bed. Fingers handcuffs. Not knowing who they're for. Never to know. Push him roughly on to the bed. Face down. Biting neck, back, shoulders, ass. Unbuckle him from under me. Freed to the knees. Smiling olive globes, kneaded, worked apart. Lovingly spat upon. Thick white spit shines his greasy asshole. A vision of South American virgins offered up in ritual sacrifice dances in the distance. Force my spear tongue like a knife up his hole. Bitter-sweet hollow. Turn him over, gently grab his teenage prick. Slow choke it. Twisting. Lick. bite, suck, lick. Salt. Gold.

Pull off my clothes. Climb on top, his arms pinned back. Welterweight body, partially exposed. Hips to nipples. Delicious. Slow grind. Just enough friction to make him come all over my belly. Force his fat lips against me. Sucking up his come. Watch it run down his chin. Run his chin down to my clit. Make him lick. Suck. Bite. Lick. Salt. Gold. Sucking his mouth into my cunt. Which he holds open with two fingers. Spreading the swollen bitch. Poking his hungry pink tongue into hungry pink pussy. I come as he chews me like a rabid little pig.

Want his cock. Slender prick slickly shoved inside me. He precision pumps my cunt. A manic drill. I squeeze him inside, tighten my grip. Close my legs. Focus my pussy on the ridge of his dick, the underside of its head. The smooth skin stretching. Ready to burst. Thrashing up to him, pumping myself off. Using his prick as divining rod.

I bite his shoulder, his neck, his lips. Telling him to come. I wanna see him come all over himself. Again. To come with me. To make me come. He sprays all over the both of us, swearing in Spanish. Eyes closed. Jerking spastically as I bang my clit, slapping it, pinching it. Pulling myself off. Pushing him off of me. Telling him he's got to go.

New York acts as a flame to which every moth eventually freaks. Second and third generation Eastern Europeans. Immigrant Chinese. Exiles from the Middle East. Haitians. Cubans. Puerto Ricans. Southern Blacks. Italians. Russians. Koreans. Kids from the Midwest, the Bible Belt, the suburbs. Executives from Connecticut. Producers from the Hamptons. Musicians from New Jersey. Failed actors from the Motor city. Would-be models fresh off the farm. A bizarre fondue, all consumed with a sickness to succeed. To beat the odds. Turn their life around. Win at any cost. Oblivious to the atrocious exchange rate. Regardless of the toll. In spite of the obstacles. Despite the quality of living. The shitty tenement apartments. Ridiculous rents. Poor working conditions. Contamination. Decay. Ripe with sick twists trolling for night highs.

The beautiful reptilian creature began to puke, hanging her head between the twin beds. A violent retching produced copious explosions. An oatmeal consistency, brightly coloured in every shade of curry, puddled on the hotel carpeting. I continued to spank her ass in rhythm with her expulsions. Too drunk to stop.

My male cohort, a drunken musician, was admonishing me for showing no respect for the sick. I snickered, "She's not sick, she's just too high..." as I continued to slap, pinch, bite her lushly plump ass cheeks. It was no worse than what he'd done to me on any number of occasions. We'd get together once every few weeks, consume enough Jack Daniels to stimulate blind rage and fuck each other's brains out. It was fine by him, when I was the object of distorted lust, but he couldn't bear paying witness to his own abuse employed on a third party. Maybe he was just pissed off over the fact that our lithe lesbian plaything had agreed to accompany us to our room, under the condition that she should not be penetrated. Anything else, to me, seemed fair game. He lost it when my hand was replaced by my belt, welting glorious patterns on her ripe buttocks. He rushed me, tackling me off the bed, both of us landing in the thick, stinky puddle whose still steaming heat felt almost erotic. His huge frame, well padded with the remnants of baby-fat and alcohol bloat, made it impossible to escape from the two-foot wide prison I was wedged in between the two beds. He smothered my mouth with his massive hammy fist, smearing a small trail of her puke on my cheek. He whispered, slurring, "Lay off her. Pick on someone your own size." He outweighed me by sixty pounds. I gently reached under him, deadlocking his porky cock and balls. Twisting. He was so drunk, he mistook it for foreplay. Covering my mouth with his stale cavity, deep throating me with his pickled tongue. I sucked.

He stood up, hoisting me with him. He was one of the few men who could actually fuck with more mastery the more fucked up he was. Straight, he was useless. Blind drunk, one of the best, awesomely powerful. With one hand he released the beast below his belt. With the other he ripped my flimsy pants off, the silky fabric scratching me tender. He grabbed me under both knees, lifting me high up in the air like a small toy. Slamming me down onto his prick, sticky from our little wrestling match. With brute strength exaggerated by the alcohol, he pummelled us into a mutual orgasm, throwing me down when he was done, onto one of the twin beds. Wagging his finger at me as he left the room, he instructed me not to fuck with her, she, who was still racked with dry heaves, spasming on the adjoining bed. I lied and promised I'd let her sleep it off. Throwing a glass or two at the door the second he walked out. Typical prick couldn't stand to see his own tricks employed elsewhere.

I returned my attentions to the fine chubby ass still clenching and releasing itself in spastic rhythm. Beating at it now with my shoe. As if punishing her for the heroin/alcohol cocktail whose evil effects continued to rack her body. The spasms slowly subsided, rendering a rather fetching stupor. "Enough, please," she managed to mutter, excusing herself to the bathroom. Dragging pale white feet over the trail of broken glass she was too stoned to feel. She would tomorrow, a memento of an evening when all other details were blurred. It's always easier to remember that which pains, especially when the physical scars sing testament to a blurry recollection.

I had often been accused of latent misogyny. Usually after misguided threeways. The men involved, recognizing my masculine tendencies, were seemingly disturbed when forced to witness their own reflections. In truth, I did enjoy abusing women, but no more than I myself enjoyed being abused... One male friend went so far as to warn me of the possibility that one day I would actually murder another woman if I wasn't extremely careful – if I didn't watch out. He was fearful that my obscene fascination with Ted Bundy, Ricky Ramires, and Richard Speck would worm its way into my psyche with the most disturbing of consequences. He reasoned that I was merely trying to kill the woman inside myself, that part of me that had borne the brunt of prolonged incest, whose unresolved pain had manifested itself in sadism, paedophilia and nymphomania. That through sexual abuse and humiliation, I was merely reliving again and again my own torture. I insisted he drop his faulty Krafft-Ebing prognosis, that pleasure was always piqued by small dollops of pain, and I would never do to another woman what I wouldn't encourage done to myself. Besides, if I were to actually take the trouble to murder, there were far too many men much more deserving. Like himself. That killed the conversation. Again, horrified to see himself painted in the mirror in front of him.

Long walks sucking up every inch of the city. Stalking the vibrancy of certain blocks, whose lonely stoops I would haunt under night's shadow. 2nd Street between A and B. Delancey Street below Chrystie. Rivington. The West Side Highway. 37th Street in Hell's Kitchen. East 116th. 110th at Central Park Upper Broadway. Sneak into hallways, basements, onto the roof. Down the fire escapes. Eavesdrop through door frames on dinner conversations, drug deals, arguments, cooing, crying children. Decoding the building's history from overheard stories.

Fascinated by the frequency with which the atmosphere would alter. Every few feet, consumed by a different texture, taste, smell. An urgency. The city itself a vampire, a massive sucking vortex. Feeding on you, coaxed through its side streets. Another ghost in the machine. A whisper on the radar screen. An invisible star passing through a dead man's galaxy.

I was introduced to Johnny by mutual friends. He was up for the weekend from St Petersburg, Florida. Accompanied by his childhood sweetheart, a hot ditzy blonde who spoke in baby talk, dressed as kinderwhore, and drove me up the fucking wall. By the end of their two day visit I had already engaged her in a brutal cat fight, which split her lip and blackened her eye, and fucked him in the bathroom of the same bar where the brawl took place, sealing my victory as I wrangled him away from her. Yeah, what a fucking prize he was. Full-blooded Irish iron worker, full-blown alcoholic with serious case of Brando damage, fuelled by narcissistic rage. Played every scene as if the cameras were rolling, caught up in his Hollywood dreamscape. Which made it nearly impossible to focus your attention anywhere but in his direction. He put on more of a show than I did. Had to have him.

Johnny sent Jeanie packing back to Florida. Convinced we were the love story of the century, a classic couple in the Burton/Taylor tradition. He connived one of his St Pete buddies to take us in for a few months, until he found work, and we could sort out our own rat trap. Bunked with the gay antique dealer occupying the back bedroom so small only a fold-out cot and a thirteen-inch black and white TV had any breathing space. Spent nights at filthy old men's bars, hustling 8-ball for a deuce a pop. Scoring seconals at the clinic on 2nd Avenue, we'd wash 'em down with cheap vodka, play a few games, pick up some chump change and screw for hours waiting for the grey waves of static snow to appear on the screen in the corner of the room which lulled us into unfit sleep.

8-ball kept us full of alcohol and cigarettes, but we weren't making any leeway with the supposed rent we owed, nor the money we were trying to scramble up to get our own place. Johnny suggested I get up my own hustle, could make a lot more money for a lot less work, if I was willing to throw a little pussy down. Didn't tell him I was ahead of the game. Had a few regulars who I already milked with sex for dollars. He was too jealous. Okay if he thought of it, he'd go ballistic if he knew I'd already been there.

We had fifteen bucks left. Enough for a couple of sandwiches, small bottle of Smirnoff and a pack of Marlboros. Hiked up to Midtown on the East side.

Stuck my thumb out. The fourth passing car pulled over. Sixty-some-year-old black man in a faded caddy. Lied and said 2nd and St Marks hoping to steer the conversation our way. Didn't take long till we settled on fifty bucks and a cheap motel in Jersey. The old man pulled out a few joints of decent Jamaican which he lit on the other side of the Hudson Tunnel. Went to a place he knew, tucked off the main drag, called The Rite Spot. Pity the fool that went there for shut-eye. Three out of the ten rooms vibrated with the vagrant sounds of someone else's nightmare. I was about to enter into my own. The pot and vodka took the edge off. Needed it to.

The dingy room smelled of lysol and roach spray. A

faint undercurrent of bathroom mildew mingled with disinfectant. At least the bed was clean, a lop-sided queen-size complete with brown, floral patterned quilt which looked like a leftover from a Jersey garage sale. Johnny gravitated to the TV set. Nursing the vodka while fucking with the old black and white's antennae, trying to tune in an old episode of Felix The Cat. "Big John", the john, settled himself in the centre of the crumbling bed and with a wink motioned me over. I blessed him with the most innocent smile I could conjure, extending my open palm in his direction. He slipped the money in my hand, closing my fingers around the crumpled fifty. Gave my wrist a dainty kiss with thick lush lips the colour of aubergines. Pulled me on top of thick girth which swelled with each breath like an over-inflated beach ball. Big hard belly to bounce against. Fat, dry fingers made rough with work grabbing handfuls of plump ass. Baritone voice whispering instructions, encouragements. Black eyes bloodshot, but full of spunk and sparkle.

I removed his shoes, slipping them beside the bed. Helped him out of his pants, folding them over the plastic chair near the window. Felt like he deserved a little pampering. Hard working old man with an eighth grade education, who raised himself up and out of the slums of Trenton, scrimping and saving with his wife of thirty-three years to open a dry cleaning business in Newark a few years back. Hard luck story with a middle income ending. Treated himself to a girl now and then 'cause the wife just couldn't keep up with him any more. Arthritis. I could barely keep up. Pulled out every trick I knew. Sucked and fucked him till I was raw, worked his prick every way I could. Still wouldn't come. Big John was making sure he got his money's worth.

There were three minutes left on his hour. Johnny

had turned away from the set and for the last twenty minutes was stroking himself off, watching me work on Big John. I was between his legs, ass stuck in the air, tonguing huge balls whose fragrant perfume of African Musk, baby powder and Zest made me swoon. A dizzying aroma whose intoxicating aerosol filled the entire room in a unique bouquet. He smelled of perfect sex.

His huge paws encircled the purple head, twisting foreskin up and over. Then down and around, exposing a delicate pink under the prick's ridge. The black shaft, fat with excitement, being tortured mercilessly with a frenzied squeeze. Shiny sac lapped at, slurped on, sucked in, nearly swallowed until the low belly moan of near orgasm grumbled, tumbling out from between clenched teeth. He exploded all over my face and hair, crying out for Jesus, Mercy, Mary and Joseph, gluey white gruel which smelled of bleach, the beach. Johnny came too, pulling my face around to catch a second coating of sea-spray on lips and nose.

Big John gave us a ride back in to the city. Gave me his card with the number from the dry cleaners on it. Told me to call when I was strapped for cash. We'd work something out. We made a date to meet the following Friday. I talked him in to lending me a small advance. I found an apartment on East 12th, only seventy-five bucks a month. Needed a down payment. He peeled off a baker's dozen in twenties. Sweet trick.

The apartment was in a back building, its courtyard on either side of the entrance piled high with garbage. The result of fires on both sides of the six-storey brick shithouse. Insurance arson. No-one else saw fit to move into the dark brown cave, whose last tenant had committed suicide by electrocuting himself with the television set. His dead body lay rotting for days, his face turned into dog-food by his only companion, a rabid German Shepherd whose tongue at first tried to resuscitate before hunger and teeth took over. The spark from the TV had burned a small black hole in a paint-by-numbers African Mambo scene. The dead stain on the floor left its ghostly mark even after two coats of fresh paint. Nothing could kill the smell of death which seemed to waft in at odd intervals. When the afternoon sun swelled, so did the smell. A Santeria Botanical on Avenue B recommended a small glass bottle, illustrated with crude skull and cross bones, "POISON" stamped in blood red child's scrawl. The stooped old woman who ran the store assured me through broken English, that yes, even the stench of death would magically disappear if I used three drops, three times a day for three days. She was right. It was the only curative.

Johnny got his own gig hustling 'dates' at a queer escort service that specialized in S/M. That lasted until he got a little too turned on by a submissive trick who thought he wanted to have the shit kicked out of him. Until he did. The trick threatened to press charges, but couldn't risk the exposure. Worked as a security guard at the Court House. Couldn't stir up too much shit. Suffered through the fractured collar bone collecting sick leave and kept his fucking mouth shut. End of job. Johnny went back to hustling pool, petty thieving and small-time blackmail. He'd pick up on octogenarian men or women, trick with 'em once or twice and weasel enough information out of them to be bought off in bribes. We somehow managed to pay the bills, eat occasionally, stay constantly stoned on seconals and drink religiously. What else was there to do?

His violent sexuality landed me in hospital on more than one occasion. We had been lying in bed quietly arguing about my girlfriend Connie. Johnny swore I wanted to fuck her, had fucked her. He could smell her on me. I told him to stop dreaming, he was far too romantic, to fuck off, and besides, what the fuck did it matter, what fucking business of HIS, was it, who I was or wasn't fucking? Oh, it was fine if I fucked geriatric black men to pay the rent, but I wasn't allowed to play with my girlfriends. To this he took great offence. Stabbed me once, casual as popping a beer can. Just reached over and stuck it in. I didn't even see it coming. Didn't even feel it go in. It wasn't till he pointed out to me that I was bleeding, that I had a fucking clue. He had punched me in the left side of my belly, a closed fist lanced around a thin stiletto. Didn't even feel it. A stupid momentary rage bathed in pathos. Then he handed me the knife. Weak smile on twisted lips. I had my chance, could have laid him out right then and there. Could have gotten away with it. Self-defence. Domestic abuse. Crime of passion. Justifiable homicide. Involuntary manslaughter. Had my chance to taste his death. Let him live, fool.

I stuffed a pair of white cotton boxers into the small bloody hole three inches from my navel. Floral patterns blossomed in bright red. We got dressed and walked the twenty-odd blocks to Bellvue, fresh out of cab fare. Sad tin cans rattled a sick little ditty. The only song that broke the eerie still of pre-dawn. I started to trail little tears of blood for blocks before we reached the Emergency Room. I wondered if thirsty sparrows would sup on my life force. Imagined dogs' bloody paw prints leading helter skelter up 2nd Avenue. We picked up the pace, both of us still in a seconal-induced stupor. The reason for our calm. After the storm.

The Emergency Room was dead empty. Unusual for Bellvue, a crumbling roach-infested throwback, part psychiatric prison, welfare hostel, VA stronghold. Hard to tell the patients from the doctors. All vacantly wandering the massive labyrinthine halls in manic drug-induced torpors. I had been there many times before. Visiting friends who had voluntarily checked themselves in to take advantage of the unlimited supply of mood-altering drugs, or to de-tox from mood-altering drugs. Or simply to be supervised before further hurting themselves or anyone else. At the time, whether it was City-run or not, you could always receive treatment at Bellevue, no matter how broke you were. Of course, the quality of the treatment was questionable at best. The last time I had been there, a mad Russian Jew, claiming to be an MD had performed cryosurgery on me, cauterizing with nitrogen what he had assessed as pre-cancerous cells growing on my most sensitive nerve centres. I still believe it was just a ploy to make me suffer for what he perceived as my terminal indiscretion. His scaly face leering as he hopscotched back and forth under the hose inserted into my body, grumpily exclaiming "It's going to be much more painful if we are forced to operate...", his wet mouth twitching in glee as I writhed in agony.

I collapse at the front desk, clutching my belly. Cascades of wet red staining the yellowed linoleum. The head nurse rushes over trying to staunch the flow with snowy gauze. Takes one look at Johnny and decides to separate us, forcing him to wait in the visiting room while she ushers me into a dirty cubicle, littered with the bloody remains of a just released casualty, victim of random gunplay. The doctor stumbles in unshaven, crusty, suffering from lack of sleep, caffeine jitters and a pounding migraine. Inspecting the wound he questions how, why. I lie and say attempted robbery, hoping somebody else isn't in the lobby questioning my amour. After deep swabs to my bloody gash, he shoots the area with a local anaesthetic and proceeds to stitch it closed. A quarter inch more and my pancreas would have been punctured.

I ask for some pain killers, although strangely enough I still don't feel any pain. Seconals still coursing through my blood stream. I lie and tell him I'm allergic to codeine and tylenol, hoping for something stronger. It works. The nurse escorts me back to the lobby where Johnny's being questioned by two men in blue. I hear him feign ignorance, claiming he just walked me over. I butt in and give the cops a standard lie, two black junkies looking for quick cash, didn't have any, so they stabbed me. They let it slide. All stabbings, shootings, attacks of random violence are subject to police scrutiny. Yeah, right, sixty-two seconds of questioning and the case is closed.

The garbage between the front and back building seemed to ebb and flow. A couple of middle-aged bums had taken up camp in the firebombed remnants of the tenements flanking either side of my apartment. Shadows from candlelight would perform ghoulish dances under the night sky. The scent of kerosene lamps, their greasy pungency mingling with the neighbours' rice and beans lent a third world smell to the new, ten foot-high pile of trash stewing in the courtyard. The old Puerto Rican widow on the third floor had painted a pink crucifix on her door, frightened by recent events. First the suicide of the previous tenant whose apartment Johnny and I now inhabited (our presence alone enough to warrant curses), then the bums, then the rumours spread by the landlady who claimed to have seen giant snakes, massive boa constrictors, slithering through the landfill of debris. The landlady never thought to simply have the junk hauled away. Her apartment itself, a testimonial to trash collection. Every surface, including the prerequisite bathtub in the kitchen, was loaded ceiling-high with old TV guides, *Variety*, *The New York Post*, cereal box tops, record covers, coupons, clippings, cut-outs, clothes, mail correspondence, empty tissue boxes, cracked plates, bent

Lydia Lunch

silverware, hairbrushes, nail-clippers, coke cans, and candy-bar wrappers. In short, a total pigsty. Haven for roaches. Johnny and I had been cooped up in our cave for a couple of months. The honeymoon was on the wane. We were driving each other nuts. His hot Irish temper, maniacal jealousy, rampant voyeurism driving me crazy. He couldn't stand me turning tricks unless he came along. Hated it when I'd sneak out with my girlfriend Connie, but wanted to hear every detail. Loved watching me get fucked by every prick that made me itch so he had something to yell at me about. Horrible arguments turned into foreplay.

One lazy summer night I decided to run down to the corner store to refuel our supplies. Marlboros and vodka. A couple cans of coke. Hershey bar or two. He was pissed when I refused to change before leaving the house. It was fine if I wanted to flaunt myself in all manner of provocative dress, as long as he was leading the parade. But dare I depart the fetal cave in simple black mini and thigh-high boots without him, I was doomed to interminable discussions whose frenzied ravings would rattle the rooftops.

One night just to piss him off even further after yet another ridiculous tirade, I slammed the door and ran across the street to fuck the Jewish/Puerto Rican jazz musician who I'd been stalking since we'd first moved in. Quick thirty-minute fuck and suck.

Upon returning I found Johnny passed out on the floor. Two empty bottles of seconals washed down with a fifth of Smirnoff. No idea how many caps he had swallowed. Didn't know whether it was just a drunken attempt to impress, that perhaps he had only taken a few and hid the rest, hoping to incur sympathy, or a melodramatic suicide attempt, in keeping with the apartment's tradition.

Cold water splashed in his face. Deep kicks to his kidneys. The slapping of both cheeks. Banging his head against the floor. Nothing I did could rouse him. Not even a flutter of eyelash. I ran out of the apartment, down the six flights, running for three or four blocks before I could find a payphone whose receiver was still attached. I dialled 911, gave the address. They told me to go wait outside. They'd arrive within the hour. I screamed into the mouthpiece that by that time he might already be dead. Or even worse, brain dead. The weary operator insisted there was nothing more she could do. She placed the call. I'd just have to wait.

I ran back upstairs to check on Johnny. Who had already turned a sickly hue. I was so fucking mad at him, I stood over his near corpse cursing the son of an Irish bitch. Screaming at him to wake up, get up, before I fucking killed him. I wanted to fucking kill him. I should have fucking killed him. But I couldn't. I loved him too much. Loved his evil, sleazy grin. His greasy demeanour. His long skinny legs. His big, nasty dick. His cruelty. His jealousy. His insanity. How insane he made me. His perversion.

(A horrible incident. Two weeks before we'd met. He had to be inoculated for a virulent strain of canine gonorrhoea. Which he had picked up while fucking his friend's dog on a bet. Won twenty-five dollars. The doctor's visit and shots cost double. I loved his sickness.)

The ambulance pulls up sirens blaring. I run downstairs to summon them. The neighbourhood kids surround it as if it's the Good Humour Truck. They grumble when I warn the attendants that we're on the top floor. Complicates their procedure. We rush upstairs. They take vital signs, barking out orders, questions. Radio into the hospital. Bellevue. Strap him to the plywood stretcher. Halfway down the six flights, one of the attendants pauses to brush a cockroach from his shoulder. It fluttered down

Lydia Lunch

from the ceiling. This causes a pile-up from the rear which sends Johnny and the contraption he's strapped to bouncing down ten or twelve steps. Face turning mushy against the bannister. If it wasn't so horrible it would have been funny.

They wheeled him into the ICU amidst the ear-splitting din of a Friday night's pandemonium. Every plastic seat in the Emergency room occupied. Screaming children, laughing and hysterical, gathered around puddles of congealing blood. Dirty little feet, some barefoot, others in summer sandals or running shoes, make a mosaic in scarlet red. Their mothers making the sign of the cross, fingering prayer beads, cursing and crying for the salvation of the fathers. Victims of stabbings, gunshots, lurid accidents, bar-room brawls, foolish bravado. Dirty looks shot at my back, as we're rushed straight through, no time left for the preliminary of endless paper work. That can wait till morning. Now it's time for the stomach pump. A horrendous attempt at intervention from death's doorstep. As soon as the doctors have Johnny stabilized, they advise me to go home, get some rest. As if I could sleep. I stupidly take up silent vigil surrounded by the wounded and long waiting. The wailing of old women finally lulls me like siren song into unsound sleep. At 6.00A.M. there's still no word whether Johnny will recover or remain semi-vegetative. At this point I wish he would just die. Be dead and done with it. Not wake up. Meet his maker, that retired iron worker in the sky, whose battered Irish face, like Johnny's own, is sprinkled with pale freckles, luminescent green eyes both cruel and playful. I wonder if in his coma, he's finally at peace. No longer struggling, no longer fighting in himself what he hated in his father, yet turned out to emulate. I imagine a spidery cocoon clouding consciousness with a bear hug's embrace. Bliss.

Thirty-six hours later he wakes up. A groggy smile,

he asks for a cigarette. A coke. Wants to go get a hamburger. Starts to dismantle the I.V., various tubes and monitors which he's hooked up to. A young, green candy-striper rushes over admonishing. Tells him he can't do that. He lets slide a sleepy, sidelong grin and says "Sure I can. Don't tell anybody." Gives a wicked little laugh, impish. Irresistible. "I'm checking myself out. Wanna come?" She shrugs and runs off looking for the head nurse. Johnny slips into his jeans, tight black T-shirt and unlaced converse. "Did you miss me?" he whispers, snuggling into my neck, scooping me up, plopping me on the hospital bed. I mouthed back "Yes, baby, I missed you," not meaning a single fucking word. I wished he was dead.

Most of the men I have lived with have attempted suicide at least once. I was always disappointed that none of them actually succeeded. I secretly wished them all dead at one time or another. Longed for the badge of widowhood. A reason to mourn their passing. Wished they had the guts to go through with it. Angered by their pathetic plea for attention. Intervention. Always believed suicide was the brave man's way out. The ultimate gamble. Definitive Fuck You. That there were justifiable reasons for suicide. Any coward can live, cowering for years under the bullshit. The agony. The pain. Self-inflicted or not. It was the weaklings who kept sticking their chins out. To be pummelled again and again. Under the heavy weight of a karmic bruise. Some souls were born to be forever tortured in this life. Never to find peace. Relief. Sanctuary. Never to be released from the burden of their heredity. Bad genetics. Battered psyche. Tortured libido. Fractured ego. Twisted id. Shattered nerves. Adrenal chaos. Their torture a springboard for torturing others. Victim becomes victimizer. Could suicide throw a kink into the transgenerational link through which the family tradition of psychotic behaviour was bred?

Our relationship took a serious nosedive with Johnny's recovery. Violent arguments would escalate into physical battery. With him as recipient. I took to sleeping with a knife under my pillow for precaution anyway. Alcohol blurred reason, turning minor squabbles vicious. He'd accuse me of instigating petty indiscretions that he had orchestrated. Then turn around and sodomize my dire enemy, a catty Oriental dominatrix on the floor of the same bathroom we had first made it in. One of us would start an argument, but he was always the first one out the front door, heading down to the local old man's bar to cool off. When I tried to leave first, he'd chain me to the kitchen sink with handcuffs. One time he came back dusty from head to toe. Claiming to have been waiting for the LL train to run him over. He fell asleep on the tracks. A bum pulled him to safety as the train was entering the station. His whole life was a series of near misses. He was proud of a stunt he had pulled off in Florida that went out over the Associated Press wire. He had climbed to the top of a huge power transformer, transistor radio in hand blaring Doo Wop. Cigarette pack rolled into his sleeve, extra Brylcreem to keep his hair in place. Supposedly just to have a think, smoke a cigarette. Someone called the police, fearing he was going to jump. The cops called the fire station, who called the ambulance. Who all arrived simultaneously, sirens blaring. He laughed once he figured out they were there for him. The cops tried to coax him down easy, words of encouragement cooed through a bullhorn. All he wanted was a cigarette. Trouble is, he forgot his lighter. Twenty feet from the ground, he called down to one of the cops asking for a match. Smirking. As soon as he hit terra firma, the cop punched him in the jaw, put him in an armlock and handcuffed him behind his back. He was taken away on trespassing charges. The AP wire reduced the entire episode to a blurb which read "Request for last cigarette as suicide attempt is foiled by St Pete Police."

Typical Johnny.

After every horrendous argument, Johnny on a peace-keeping mission would bring home another animal. A futile attempt at pacifying the demise of my tolerance. First came a huge white rabbit, whose cute, yet idiotic demeanour could diffuse even the most irritable of moods. Until it started to piss on the bed. Then a cat for the rabbit to play with, maybe it was lonely, hence the bedwetting. The rabbit would often beat the shit out of the cat, kicking it relentlessly with strong hind legs, a cheery glee etched on its stupid face. Like my own, when physically taunting Johnny. Followed by a skink, iguana and gecko, whose bumpy flesh shared the chameleon's talent for infusing itself in various disguises. Left out of its cage to roam freely, the gecko turned home exterminator, devouring every last spider, fly and roach. A helpful low-rent pet that every New Yorker should invest in.

Next, a four foot-long Burmese python, whose projected growth might one day reach twelve feet. A possessive creature spoiled on slithering under my clothes, seeking much-needed body heat. I'd sleep with it wrapped around my arms or legs, safe from Johnny in its protective embrace. Its slow languid movements a tonic for stress. Irritation.

To feed the snake, we started to breed mice. Cheaper than visiting the pet store, who were already into us for crickets, cat food, rabbit pellets, flea spray, room deodorizers and scratch posts.

The amount of time and energy necessary for the upkeep of such a motley menagerie took nothing away from our now daily bickering. We'd argue about money, sex, drugs, the weather. Johnny landed a job with a construction company assembling condos on the upper East side. He complained about the hours, the other workers, the boss, the management, the pay. Spoiled from his gig in Florida where as the union leader's son, he could come and go as he pleased, and still pull in seventeen-fifty an hour. With no clout at the new job, he was reduced to showing up on time and working as hard as everybody else. A slight unbearable for such a fragile ego. He'd come home half plowed, encouraging me to imbibe in his favourite drink, the Ashtray, a shot of vodka slipped inside the neck of a Budweiser. I used alcohol as a firestarter to enhance whatever pills I was popping. Alone I found it boring, bloating, dull. His last overdose wasted our stash of seconals. Which I was still pissed about. The doctor at the 2nd Avenue clinic cut us off after being contacted by the staff at Bellevue, curious about the prescription. My sobriety rubbed Johnny the wrong way. He accused me of being intolerant, bitchy, cold, a cunt. I was. Drunk, he was affectionate, happy, sweet, until about the fifth drink. The brutish sailor would emerge. Full of destructive urges whose targets were usually my possessions. I took to storming out of the house, by now bored of his infantile tantrums. One night after rejecting his drunken advances and being accused of being both a frigid bitch and a flaming whore, I took shelter at a girlfriend's house. When I returned the next morning, sure he'd already be at work, the entire apartment was destroyed. The bed had been set on fire, a small hole still smouldering weakly, curtains and blinds ripped from their rods, trunks of clothes turned upside down, rifled through, left in tatters. Holes punched in the walls with bizarre messages scrawled, arrows pointed into the gaping maw with "Help me I'm in here", "Brother can you spare a drink?", "I love how you hate me", scribbled in black magic marker. And all the animals, save the snake, killed in a senseless bloody rampage. All the mice had their eyes poked out. The lizards were beheaded. The cat skinned. The rabbit trussed up like a turkey dinner, already roasted, set out on a platter on the kitchen table. Years later I was to find out he actually gave the rabbit skins to a friend of mine, who used them as decoration on a small drum kit. I packed a small bag, rifled through his dirty clothes for money. He had just been paid. Three hundred and seventy-six dollars in his pocket. I left him a ten-spot and headed to the airport. Blew the Iranian cab driver in exchange for the forty dollar fare.

Los Angeles, an endless sprawl of suburban subdivisions spread out in a massive grid encircling Hollywood, the fraudulent Mecca of egotistical schemers. Everyone's got a grift in Hollywood, or working hard on devising one. The city is paved with broken hearts, shattered dreams, dashed hopes. Everyone expects their fifteen minutes, not realizing their minor brush with greatness will pollute the rest of their tortured lives, creating an almost unbearable torment whose mantra cries out for what could have been, what should have been, what will never be.

Its history of random violence, drive-by shootings, highway snipers, serial killers, religious cults, countless casualties, revolves around the eternal possibility that something greater is almost within reach of every leech, loser and low-life. Hollywood has created Sodom with the help of a corporate machine that feeds on the bruised bones of sacrificial offerings. Its obscene wealth, undeserved fame, untold riches reside side by side with a desperate poverty whose scope is forever overlooked, avoided, ignored. The root of all the sickness swelling inside its soured belly.

I went out to L.A. with a dream on my sleeve too. A dream of escaping the asshole who was obsessing my life

---

back in New York. Just a small vacation, three or four days to clear my head. I put a call in to Pleasant, a hot Hollywood fixture. Part belly dancer, all ghost of Jayne Mansfield. A luscious redhead who knew where to score what from who, whenever. I knew her from New York, a friend of a friend. Suggested she shake some titty at the Wild West Saloon. Even lent her some panties. She thought she was returning the favour when she suggested I hit a party that was happening on my first night in the City of Lights. Told me to look for Marty; a speedway freak who played hairdresser by day down in Malibu. She claimed he was my type, which I took to mean a little bit twisted. Said he grew up in Topanga, had a thing for Charlie, surrounded himself with chicks with Sexy Sadie fantasies. She was sure I'd be amused.

The party was a bust, full of Valley chicks, jocks and rockabillies. Disappeared into the kitchen looking for something stronger than liquor. There was a small bowl of quaaludes propped demurely behind a jar of powdered vitamin C. I popped one, stuck three in my pocket for later. After all, I was going to be out there for a few days.

Someone cranked the stereo up a few notches, the strains of early Carl Perkins wobbled the posterboard walls. I could see a wide circle form in the living room, as a greasy biker took centre stage and slicked his hair back, threw one hip forward and began a hilariously awful Elvis impersonation. I knew it must be Marty. The gathering crowd clapped along, encouraging obscene gyrations, offset by hoots and howls. I was vaguely repulsed.

I decided to check out the master bedroom and bath, in search of a small token to justify my journey. A small tray of cheap jewellery sat on the dresser, I bypassed that and opened the top drawer. More costume crap and a fat rubber band of credit cards. I popped the Mastercard into my pocket, more as a memento. Rifled through the bathroom cabinets. Slipped a handful of ten milligram valium into my pocket. Felt much better. Thought I'd return and make the rounds once more before departure. Opened the bathroom door to find Marty cleaning his nails with a small switchblade. "Axle grease," he admitted under his breath. I could smell it on him. It turned me on. Like the smell of gasoline. Like my first real fuck with some blond-haired blue-eyed kid whose father was a two-bit mechanic in Upstate. "I'll be right back," he whispered undoing his belt buckle, a tarnished grim reaper. I headed out to the balcony, figuring he'd come looking.

I scanned the L.A. skyline, a neon blur of late night commerce. Scattered numbers in my head trying to size up the population, wondering how many dollars were spent every minute in vulgar pursuit of the next big thing, big star, major motion picture, scam, scheme, rip-off, rape. Wondering how many living rooms were under siege by drunken day labourers taking out the boss's bullshit on the wife and kids, how many punches were being thrown in alleys at the back of dirty bars, how many shots were being fired from Mexican gang bangers, how many kids were undergoing their first hustle with some stinking john in any make of car cruising down Hollywood Blvd, Santa Monica Blvd, Crenshaw Blvd.

I didn't hear him come out. Felt his breath on the back of my neck. "Creepy Crawl?" he questioned, an invitation I knew I somehow, somewhere would take him up on.

Marty was a mongrel mix of Cherokee/Black Irish. Trouble, in other words. He spoke in a strange dialect more Blue Ridge Mountains than Southern Californian. Spent his formative years racing dirt bikes in the backyard of the

Manson Family down in the snakepit of Topanga Canyon. Watched the mudslides come and go, wiping out the hippies, hillbillies and dirt farmers who had set up camp in ill-constructed shacks which formed the valley near enough to Malibu, yet still light years away. Said he stayed there because he respected Mother Nature's mean streak, and besides what's a little mud. The place he shared with his brother, a lowbrow surf freak, had just withstood four feet of thick sludge seeping in and back out of its four shit-stained walls. Said he'd move when the place collapsed. I dug his gumption. Easy going nature. Devil may care attitude. Invited him to my hotel the next night, told him to come by when he was through re-styling the hair of would-be B-movie actresses who frequented the upscale yet still gritty salon he managed four days a week a few blocks from the beach.

I prepared for our date by swallowing a couple of quaaludes washed down with Jack Daniels. I slipped into sheer black, applied some lipstick, put on my pumps while dimming the lights. Opened the door, hair-line fracture crack, popped a matchbook flap under the dead bolt with "TRUE CONFESSIONS" stamped seductively in fire engine red, its 900 number torn in two. Knew he'd know exactly what to do. Stimulated myself with moistened fingertips dipped in drink. The stinging skin contracting and twitching as I twisted the tender flesh between index and forefinger. Felt so good I slipped into slumber. Woke to scissors pressed firmly to throat. The smell of hair gel and axle grease a pungent intoxicant. The mute TV transmitting a dead station whose black and white shadows tango'd upon the bed. "Will you die for me?" he purred, quoting Manson's headtrip played on Tex Watson a few months before the Tate/LaBianca murders. "I'd kill for you," I lied back, cementing the bond that would become a two year long, on

---

again/off again love/hate, white trash romance.

The sex was a blur of unpronounced threats, deadly possibilities, future recall. *Badlands, Bonnie & Clyde, The Boston Strangler, I Want To Live.* Scattered dreamscapes melting in and out of consciousness. Trapped in a timezone where minutes stretch into hours.

Woke up to find him gone. "Downstairs at 7" scrawled on the mirror in spunk.

He picked me up in a babyshit-brown '58 Ford Pickup. Cruised around Watts pulling up to Piggy's Fat Back, a Mississippi-style Bar-B-Q take-away consisting of a single battered countertop set against bullet-proof glass. The misspelled menu chicken-pecked in pencil near the low-hung, fly-specked ceiling. A tired overhead fan threatened collapse. Ordered Five Alarm pork tips, potato salad and spicy beans. The smell lingering hours after fingers are licked clean. A smell which will always remind me of his chipped, wolfen teeth, the way his hair hung down over one eye, the automatic rearranging of Levi jeans, the front of which swelled at random intervals. Our first near murder.

He asked if I'd come along on a money run. Claimed an ex-buddy was into him for twenty-five hundred. Owed him for refurbishing the tattered remains of a shell-shocked Vespa. We'd be out of there in no time. Take the money and run. Maybe stop on the way back from Inglewood to catch the late set by Eddie "CleanHead" Vincent who was doing three sets down in the Parisienne Room, a funky, rundown jazz club packed with older black couples who enjoyed a grind or two with their groove. Catch the eleven o'clock show if all went as planned.

I could smell something percolating. Knew better. Couldn't help myself. Had to see how he operated. We pulled into the underground garage, cut the lights and sat parked for a few minutes. Allowing our eyes to re-adjust. Deep breaths and a high-pitched hum from an electrical generator on the floor below book-ended the atmosphere, scattering soundwaves bouncing around in the darkness. He snuck into the glove compartment and pulled out Mr Rigid. A twelve-inch long, three-inch wide buck knife. He cleaned the blade with a soiled hanky, spat on and wiped the handle, set it in his lap. Slipped his still sticky fingers into worn leather racing gloves, picked up the buck and kissed it once for good luck. Slid it back into its sheath, snapped it onto his belt. A twisted smile from one corner of his mouth whispered "Let's do it..." Instructing me to leave the door open a crack, just enough so the light is out. Just enough for a smoother get away.

A massive hollow swallowed. Blind eyes, big cave, no fucking clue which way was even forward. Whispering "Marty... Marty..." He spat "Ssshh... c'mon..." allowing a small sliver of light to slip into the cavernous garage as he opened the stairwell door. My pulse already doing backflips. "Don't say my name again until we're back in the truck, keep your fucking mouth shut, don't even breathe hard," he threatened, spitting the words into my neck. He cocked his head toward the steps, took off up them, leaving me to lag behind, trying to get my boots to behave below my rubbered knees. Floor after floor, the hall entrances were locked. Seemed to make him more determined. He was smiling down at me as I hit level six, one hand slowly spinning the knob that allowed us entry. The other hand darting between my legs, rubbing leathered fingers against moistened jeans. He cocked his finger and pulled me into the hallway by my crotch. Eased the door shut. Holding finger to lips in a silent kiss, sniffing the remnants of nervous pussy. We found the interior stairway. Went back down to the second floor, circling around the hallway, stopped at apartment 9B. The entire Beatles *White Album* jumpcut in my head. He tried the door. Locked. Tapped boot to door jam. No answer. The lights were on, soft music lilting in the background. "Shit... we'll have to try the fire escape..." he grumbled, stroking the sheath the buck sat buckled in. I was so fucking high on adrenalin I couldn't think straight, much less make even a weak protest. I followed obediently as we once more mounted the interior stairs on the way to the roof. Just about ready to piss my pants, not knowing who we were stalking or what we would do to them once we found them. Exited onto the roof, half-moon glow, lit up with a backdrop of silver pinpricks, the irregular pattern of a dead star's radar mimicking my goosebumps. Marty slipped the door shut, pinning me against it. Unsnapped the sheath. As loud as a gunshot. Started to trace my outline, like a corpse at a crime scene, the thick blade slicing tar paper like cake icing. One hand around my throat, slow, heavy breath, hot on my face. Humid. With the tip of the blade he lifted my wrist from beside me, tracing close to my hip. Kicked my legs apart. Placed the buck between them, screwing it into the wall. Rubbed himself against the handle. Told me to close my legs, hold it in place with my pussy, make that pussy work for him. Unsnapped his jeans, shiny prick plops out, mossy aroma wafts mingling with sea breeze and gardenias, spanks it against the handle. Whimpers.

I beg for his fuck, beg to be power-slammed against the wall, squashed by his slippery prick, annihilated. Spins me against the tar paper, smooth cheek bitten by sand. Man-handles pants over ass, mutters "Ssshhh, ssshh," rubs his greasy prick between fat cheeks. Circling the bullseye.

Quick spastic jerk. Banging body parts off against twin receptors. Flood of relief as near panic is replaced with brutal focus. Slicing me open from behind like an engorged blood hound. Buck knife used as bind for breasts, steely edge flattens nipple in silent threat. Delirium.

Retreat to the pick-up. More alive the closer to Death. Our common bond a need for acceleration. Speed. Chaos. His ambition: to race dirt bikes as fast as possible on dirt tracks incurring a great many broken bones, a fractured skull, countless trips to the Emergency Room. An excuse for his behaviour. My obsession: escalate blood pressure, overstimulate adrenal glands, taunt Death. Our marriage vows: a promise to scare the shit out of each other. Apathetic assholes that we were. We thrived on fear. Fear: the greatest of all aphrodisiacs.

Marty's shack in Topanga bit it after our second date. The whole thing nearly collapsed in upon itself, burdened by a ton of mud. He salvaged some clothes, his bike and the truck. His brother escaped with the clothes on his back and a box of records. Late one night with Marty, I managed to skip out on the hotel bill. We decided to look for temporary digs, the three of us. Ended up in Venice, a block from gangland. Small dilapidated house a few blocks from the beach. I looked witchy enough to keep the local kids out of the backyard. Their older brothers away from the barred windows and doors. It was a miracle we were never fucked with or broken into. Of course there was nothing to steal. Marty had a shotgun pulled on him in front of the house early one Sunday morning, but he scared them off by warning them his blood on their hands would live to forever haunt, that the witch that he lived with would curse not only the shooter, but his entire family with spells conjured from Santeria, Voodoo and old-fashioned vengeance. That if his murder meant acceptance as gang initiation, it wasn't worth it. His whole barrio would fall. The young Mexican ran off trembling, apologizing. Tripped and fell halfway up the block, the shotgun going off, shattering the sleepy

Sunday silence. Marty sauntered in laughing, cursing racial slurs. No-one bothered us again.

I spent my days scribbling in notebooks, taking long walks down to the water, wandering aimlessly around Venice, fucking the occasional fourteen-year-old gang banger. Marty was racing once or twice a week in San Bernadino, Bakersfield, Ventura. I'd tag along like a hand maiden to a blood bath. Week after week the same ritual. Days off spent repairing his bike, recovering from the previous week's battery. Load up the truck, drive for a few hours, race for a few minutes, crash the bike, get banged up, load the bike or what was left of it back onto the truck, drive for a few more hours, recuperate. Repair the bike. Bandage the bruises, begin again.

Speedway season came to a close. Too much free time on our hands. Needed a new kick to sustain the blood rush we were both addicted to. Night drives, circling the city, suburbs, sub-divisions, outlaying communities. We'd visit old crime scenes just to zone in on the frequency. Marty seemed to know all the hot spots. The lots where the Hillside Stranglers' victims were dumped. The stomping ground of the Night Stalker. Charlie's haunts. We'd drive in silence, senses prickling the closer we'd get. He'd make up little games to test me. See if I could pick out the exact location. Insist I direct him to places I'd never been before. Question me as to how I'd get rid of the body. Would I be as bold as Buono and Bianchi and leave my victims in plain sight? Cut them up in little pieces, stuffed inside black plastic garbage bags, hurled over the side of a dumpster, or left to be picked apart by vultures in the hot California sun. Leave them to rot, perhaps undetected for days in their Hollywood Hills or Pacific Palisades or Hermosa Beach hideaways, until by chance they're discovered, bloated and swollen, a look of unrestrained horror on their death mask, found by a curious mailman, nosy neighbour, concerned relative.

Marty insisted we stained the crime site with our own markings: blood, urine, jizz, chicken bones, empty potato chip bags, match books, bottle caps, belt buckles. Any memento, offered up as ritual. Leaving personal tokens in exchange for the charge of electricity we would steal from the scene. Tapping into other realms, whose vortex could be charted by decoding latitude, longitude and astrological positions. Enthralled in lengthy discussions on geographical sickness. Los Angeles, its valleys and hillsides, thrown up by the earth's internal retching, only to once more, one day be swallowed back up by a massive earthquake which will collapse its flimsy foundations.

Merely visiting crime scenes was no longer exciting enough. We were driven to start initiating our own secret markers. Strategic locations planned out in a grid, marred by petty atrocities. A roadmap of vicious little misdemeanours whose memory we would gloat over. Arson, vandalism, dog-napping, burglary, check cashing schemes, fraud. Victimless crimes at first. Until we decided to up the ante. Until the thrill became stale and we needed that extra boost that only fear could supply. Someone else's fear.

We ended up at Al's Bar, a funky double storefront in the industrial park, just outside of downtown. Its regulars were a sloppy mix of arty locals, musicians, would-be musicians and the occasional record company minion looking for the next big thing. The odd hip tourist would wander in after squandering half a tank of gas trying to find the joint. Marty and I were ready to escalate our adventures and an unsuspecting visitor would entail both the least resistance and minimal repercussions. We spotted a drunk Australian at the bar ordering double vodkas, flashing a fat wad of cash from a snakeskin wallet. We looked at each other and chuckled. X marks the spot.

I started bullshitting with the drunkard, soliciting small chunks of information out of him. His jumbled ramblings full of boast and pomp. In town for a few days, meetings with Hollywood executives, the usual line. Told him about a hot underground club called FUCK, full of half-naked bodies engaged in outrageous acts of mutilation, fornication. If he didn't mind driving, we'd be happy to get him in. He fell for it. We had no intention of leaving the area with him. In for a little fun. At his expense.

His rental car was parked near the rear of Al's Bar. The entire neighbourhood was deserted, dark, desolate. I hopped in the front seat with the mark, Marty slithering into the backseat behind him. We drove a block or two south. I was already moist, anxious. I heard the snap pop open on the buck. Could feel Marty slicing up the back seat, long, slow slits, the soft smell of leather erupting. Marty started right in on him, confusing the lost little Aussie, asking in a filthy whisper if he liked my tits, if he'd like to screw me, if he wanted to pull over to the abandoned garage across the street, maybe get his dick sucked. Even in his drink-inspired stupor, the mark realized something was up. Too stupid to do anything about it. Still didn't notice the squealing of leather being ravaged in the back seat. Marty carving pentagrams, hieroglyphs, obscenities.

Marty became belligerent. Accusing the Australian of being queer, cheap, square, stupid. Whispering in the mark's ear, maybe he didn't even have a dick. Wouldn't have a dick... if he didn't ease the car over, give us the keys and disappear. NOW. The buck knife held firmly against his right ear, a small nick kissing a red pearl.

The mark turns to me for sympathy. Panic setting in. Bloodshot eyes full of alcohol tears. Marty cackles. Tells him he's looking in the wrong direction for mercy, pity, a hand out. Help. Insists I'm the one who instigated this ugly prank. I'm the blood sucking murder junky who loves to watch big strong men beg for their lives like tiny baby girls. If he was looking for a reason, we didn't have one. Weren't reasonable. Were never reasonable. Didn't need a reason. He was a punk mark who had insulted us with his rude refusal when offered up some fine pussy. If he was a real man... he would have been all over that shit. Marty confessing that he'd never pass up pussy... pussy was gold, man. Manna from heaven. Pussy was IT. A man that didn't worship pussy didn't value his life. Life begins with pussy, and for the lucky man it ENDS in pussy.

The idiot was already in tears. Begging us to take his wallet. He wanted us to have it, he had a couple of hundred, a few credit cards. Begging us to spare him. Offering up his watch, his boots, his leather coat. Anything but the car. He couldn't turn over the car, it was a company rental, he'd be screwed if he let that happen. I spat in his face "YOU'RE SO FUCKSTUPID... YOU DON'T EVEN DESERVE TO DIE." Not wanting to waste a perfectly good murder on this idiotic sack of shit.

Marty, grinning in the back seat, relieved him of his wallet. I felt like snatching the keys from the ignition, just to fuck with him. I let it slide. Bored with him by now. We jumped out of the car. The mark sped away. It'd take him at least a half an hour to navigate his way out of the industrial park, floundering for the exit which led to the downtown freeway. We took a small detour on the way back to the truck. Snuck inside an abandoned guard-post to kiss and grope. Heat and relief flooding the small structure as we fucked like high school students out on a first date. Laughing about the idiot's resolve to hold on to the company car. Unreal the way some people behaved. That kick kept us going for a few days. Until that old itch reappeared. An itch we couldn't resist.

We'd often wander the freeways hunting for hitch-hikers. Pick up anyone who stuck their thumb out. Stuff them into the front of the pick-up. Tight squeeze. Never had a game plan. We'd drive in silence, vibing on the possibilities. Instinctively clicking into each other's zone.

Amazed that anyone still had the fucking nerve to get inside a mobile death trap. Of course, I did it all the time. Accept rides from just about anyone. But I was different. I had a motive. Had the edge. Was prepared. Better prepared than the potential assailant. Armed with mace, the buck knife. A threat to their sanity. Teasing them with innuendo. Short skirts. Red lips. Anxious for one false move. A reason, excuse. To spray them. Stick 'em. Terrorize.

We used the map like the *I Ching*. Open to a random page. Drop the car keys. Drive. The cab of the truck, a Coney Island of the mind. A nether world of perpetual twilight. Red, white, gold lights scattershot over endless highway. Driving for miles to get nowhere. Lost, the ideal location. Trapped in a timezone where the calendar freezes. Steel cocoon. Metal womb.

Flagged down while stalking the Hollywood Hills. She jumped in front of the truck. Hysterical. Small boned black teenager. Waving frantically. Screaming for help. Dressed in waitress get-up. Pulled over, pulled her up into the front seat. Told her to calm down, stroking her hair. Two middle-aged white men abducted her at gun-point from the bus stop in front of the donut shop she worked at in Watts. Might have been cops. Threatened to shoot if she didn't suck them off. She did. Got dumped up in the hills. Asked for a ride back to the bus stop. Couldn't go home yet. Had to work on an excuse. If she told her father what happened, there'd be hell to pay. He'd go on a rampage.

We drove in silence back to Watts. Marty and I both getting off on her fear. Evil enough to consider turning back around, driving her back up to the hills and repeating her nightmare. The thought alone was enough. We dropped her at the bus stop, spent on the horrible misdeeds we had both been entertaining.

Like every other junkie, we were hooked. Poisoned on adrenalin. Addicted to it. Strung out. You up the ante and crash twice as hard the next time. Need twice as much to get off. Started making me sick. Sucking up the filthy remnants trailing fear's shadow.

Neither one of us were ready to bloody our hands by breaking the Sixth Commandment. Yet always taunting the other closer to committing the ultimate act. Even against each other. Marty would get pissed, insisting I was brainwashing him, sending secret signals, impregnating him with polluted ideas. Begging him to kill me. He'd explode from the other room, screaming at me to stop instigating... Mind fucking. Teasing. I'd play innocent. Tell him he was losing it. Didn't know what he was talking about. He was full of shit. He knew exactly what I was doing. Scaring the shit out of him. Taunting him with the vitality of my power source. A power he would have loved to consume. Forever hating himself for doing it. It was a hook. It had us both trapped.

We drove out to the desert. Something had to give. We weren't getting along any more. Spontaneity drained. Even our games were becoming predictable. Ended up at The Lost Heads Ranch. A once vital, now ruined patch of dead green. A winding dirt road, stretching endlessly, led up to the summit. Littered with rusty Chevys shot to shit with buckeye. Now roosts for prairie dogs, king snakes. Decided to park the truck, kick up a little sand. Feasting on the dry heat. Dead calm. Silence. Deep breaths. Gut swell. Fever. The horizon expanding and contracting. Heat waves.

Ripples. Then SNAP. The buck comes out. Marty tackles me, knocking me down. Sand storm. Dust devils. He kneels on top of me. Hair down over one eye. Hand to my throat. Choking. Countdown to extinction. Presses the blade to breastbone. Ready to poke. Astral high. Out of my mind. High on adrenalin. Blind with lust. Light rain from clear sky kisses face. Sweet heavenly tears sprinkle cheeks. I love you I love you I love you... whispered mantra. Marty collapses on top of me, together convulsing.

I woke up in the Emergency Room. Six scrubs in baby blue, three doctors and a couple of nurses flanking my gurney. Sugar water I.V. in one hand, stabbing the other eight or nine times with a hypodermic trying to draw blood, administer drugs to wake me up, knock me out. Evil spawn tore a hole in my tube like the return of Rosemary's Baby. Had to be cut out. Killed. Or be killed. By little fists beating to get out of my insides. Devil child, unholy terror tears a scar on Mommy's tummy, from hip to hip. We had to snatch the little wretch from his hiding spot. Tunnel dweller burrows a root up the wrong canal. Alien termination.

Nightmare in the operating theatre. Anaesthesia wears off midway through abdominal surgery. Bloody skin flaps clamped open exposing raw flesh. Vision and sound return in a scramble as I astral project over the table. Engulfed in a blanket of pain, silent shriek of prayer begging to be released from the agony of organs being scraped by the scalpel. Mute pleading to the Latin Gods of the Apothecary, "Have mercy with the ether, O Lord God on High..." No mercy is granted, as I, for what seems like hours, roam above the butchery and bloodshed pretending to catalogue my sins, beseeching every god, goddess and even the Great Dark One himself to deliver me from this endless agony. Surgical rape. Gross mutilation. A week of morphine did nothing to mask the pain of soft tissue fusing. Crawling in and out of consciousness, the sluggish stupor of fevered sleep. Vicious hallucinations. Altered dreamstates. Visions of alien abduction, insemination, vivisection. Horror.

Released. On the probation of abstinence for six weeks. The final nail in the coffin of my relationship with Marty. I couldn't stomach the thought of someone else having to take care of me. Made me bitter, withdrawn. Resentful. Blamed his evil prick for tricking one of my eggs to scramble. Couldn't stand to be looked at, touched, talked to. Wanted to be left alone, sick kitten on the corner of the bed. Left to recuperate. I asked him to split. Maybe we'd hook up again when I was functioning. Neutered I was nothing. Angered, he packed up his shit. Loaded up the truck. Took off. I hated myself for doing it. But I had to.

Like a sexually frustrated teenager, poltergeists began dancing around the house. Bizarre geometric patterns of softly coloured lights would configure around the windows and doors, warning that something or someone was either attempting to gain entry or had decided to flee. Hoping to capture release. Interior windows would self-destruct shattering into large splinters which somersaulted into the floor. The mailman had warned me of strange grey shadows hovering on the porch in front of the door. Made him too frightened to climb the three small steps. I'd have to make other arrangements to pick up my post.

Mysterious fires began to appear on the land bordering my backyard. The neighbour's dog would stand in my driveway, howling for hours, chasing its own tail in wide circles. Voices which sounded dwarfed, muffled, emanating from under my bed. I was being haunted. Probably by myself, the ghost of my aborted child signifying that it still lingered. Stubbornly clinging to the only life it knew. A netherworld of endless possibilities forever stifled.

Two weeks later I got a call from Marty's brother. He had taken off months before, unable to deal with our ongoing degeneration. Called to tell me Marty was in Intensive Care. Had crashed the truck on the Malibu Freeway. Steering column forced itself into liver, bruising kidneys, breaking ribs, smashing hip bones. Didn't know if he'd make it out. The passenger in the oncoming car wasn't so lucky. D.O.A. The driver struggling to recover from massive head trauma. Told me not to go to the hospital. Marty hadn't come out of the coma. Might never come out. Too early to predict. There was nothing I could do except wait.

Marty spent sixty-three days hooked up to tubes, monitors, machines that flushed the bruised kidneys. His liver had been severed in two. Multiple operations to sew it up, drain it out. More blood was flushed through his system than any one else in the hospital's history. He made it though. Can't kill someone that fucking stubborn. Proud of the scar that now ran from breast to pelvic bone. The parents of the other victims dropped the charges of Vehicular Homicide still pending. Said he'd suffered enough. He's still suffering. Through his third hip replacement operation all these years later. Never complained though. Not once.

Marty had a unique relationship with pain. It was almost a reminder of his existence. A safety zone where he could retreat to divest himself of all other responsibilities. Extreme physical pain elevates you to a zen-like state that shuts everything else out. It is the great divider, separating those who know how to embrace it, be cleansed by it, heal from it, almost enjoy it, from those who would shirk, avoid at any cost, wither. Die. Life-threatening injuries, numerous operations, hospitalizations, those who have been there share an uncommon bond that can never be severed.

By my early twenties I had already suffered through numerous cartilage ligament reconstructive surgeries, lymph node removals, an appendectomy, cryosurgery, an ectopic pregnancy with partial tubal ligation, and two years taunting death with Marty. We were amazed by the other's capacity to flaunt injury and smile, a badge of outrageous courage, that neither man nor machine could strip us of. Virtually indestructible. Unless you broke us up into little pieces. Which we've both been trying to do our entire lives. Spit in the devil's eye. Shit in the face of history.

Chicken-hawking teenage Cholos whose hot hands re-invigorated my energy lapse. Plotting my next move, something had to give. Night panic started setting in. Feared my Death Wish would soon overcome, sending spiralling waves of magnetic energy in a pooling vortex whose pull would reel in the wrong asshole. You can never choose your executioner. They always choose you.

Early Sunday morning, a knock on the back door. Johnny. Tracked me down through vague connections I had maintained in New York. Stupid ear to ear grin. Invites himself in. Crusty and hung over. Drove up from San Pedro where he'd been holed up hiding out from the cops. I'd heard rumours that he'd been on a two-year bender since I'd left New York. Decorated our old apartment as shrine, candles stuck in old shoes I had left behind, illuminated pictures of the two of us, hand-drawn frames etched in blood. He ended up in Southern California via Florida after a nasty incident with a middle-aged trick he had picked up in Times Square.

He wrapped the Burmese python around his neck and headed south, robbing mom and pop grocery stores, gas stations, banks in Southern Georgia, on his way back to St. Petersburg. Nickel and diming chump change to feed his heroin habit, incurred supposedly on the heels of my abrupt departure from New York. Headed west, hoping to avoid the heat.

Even wrecked, that Brando edge was spell-binding. You were afraid to take your eyes off him. No idea what he'd try to pull next. Fascinating, like a burning building, televised surgery, alien autopsy. Charmed bastard. Roadblocking harm's way.

He pulled out a small bindle of China White. I had somehow managed to avoid heroin, never done it before. Saw it take out to many assholes: years wasted on useless pursuit. Outrageous expense. Permanent stupor. Kick and kick again. Wasteful. He convinced me to take a hit. Small toke like your first joint. Knocked me flat on my ass. Passed out to wake up and puke. He stood over me laughing. Said it was the usual first response. That I'd get used to it. Learn to love the vomit. I told him to fuck off. It was my first and last experience with that shit. Never touched it again. Glad I did it though. Cured my curiosity.

Straightened out the next morning. Johnny in bed beside me. Propped up on one elbow, smirking. I had lost twenty-three hours to a somnambulant blur. Couldn't even remember if we'd fucked or not. I was still in recovery from surgery. Prayed he hadn't plowed his monstrous prick into my delicate flower. Filthy bastard. Grinning. I screamed at him to get the fuck out. Not come back. Lose my address. Split or I'd call the pigs and turn him in. He smiled sweetly, kissed my forehead, got dressed and left. Fucker.

I sold what little shit Marty and I had accumulated. All the furniture, the stereo, my books, records and most of my clothes. I had to evacuate L.A. immediately. Before I got sucked back into Johnny's bullshit. Finagled enough for a one-way ticket to Europe. Standby.

Amsterdam. A psychedelic Disneyland littered with sex shops, tattoo parlours and street after street of window after window of aging whores. Felt right at home. Pot shops on every other corner. Hundreds of cafés full of thousands of tourists, artists, would-be artists, film makers and every other form of degenerate imaginable. The influx of drunken Italians, stoned Moroccans, ignorant Americans and the loutish English made it a pickpocket's paradise.

Had the number of a DeeJay who specialized in underground music. When such a thing still existed. Met him a few years before at a performance I had pulled off at The International Theatre of Poetry and Pain. He offered me his apartment for the month of August, if I could help him meet his deadline. Organizing his yearly summer marathon, which was programmed to run in his absence. He was leaving for Thailand in thirty-six hours. Another lucky fluke.

He suggested I call Babbette. A deliciously over-ripe

avant garde film maker. Her specialty was in-depth documentaries on seventies Radicals. She had just been awarded a small grant to produce an independent feature for French TV and was looking for someone to help with all aspects of production. I signed on. Pilfering twenty per cent of the budget. Turning in a screenplay whose themes of jealousy, erotic madness, isolation and rejection were mirror images of escapades I had been orchestrating for years.

I had three weeks to pen the beast before shooting began. Three weeks to stalk the flea markets, bookshops, art galleries, after-hour clubs and drug emporiums in between manic bursts of frazzled notetaking which would be razored into the script. The filming began the day after I turned the screenplay in. A jumbled mess of raw emotion.

I met Styn on the shoot. He was in charge of special effects. Mysterious doors that opened and closed. Holes drilled into the forehead. Bloody noses. Battle wounds. I was already sleeping with two of the actors, had bedded a few of the women who catered the meals. He offered respite from the gruelling task of writing, co-directing and starring in a film that would never be seen anyway.

We'd take long breaks from the set, wandering into the wooded gulleys which flanked the massive crumbling estate in which we'd been marooned for weeks. I was endeared to his European upbringing, higher education and relaxed good manners. A different species altogether. Admitted, much like myself, to being indifferent to remorse, jealousy, guilt. Claimed the well of his emotion was a shallow pool beyond which intellect was the master. Reason took over when the heart strings swelled, sparing him the self-inflicted wounds of lost love, fractured ego, tortured relationships. A challenge to find the pocket in which he smouldered.

He'd seduce me with stolen passages from Blanchot, Bataille, Foucault. I'd escape into small monologues whose beauty filled me with ennui, melancholy. When reduced to the verge of tears, he'd laugh softly, cooing that it was time to return to work. The film was ready to wrap.

Styn suggested we celebrate, inviting me over for dinner. A second floor bachelor pad overlooking one of the many canals criss-crossing the city. Soft white lights, nondescript music, made no mention of the nightmare which was to follow. Smooth white fish, a tureen of pale soup, fruit, wine. Simple. Elegant.

Until I became nauseous. Dizzy. We hadn't even finished the meal before a small spin circled the edges of the room. My vision jellied. I was on the verge of collapsing. Drunk, but not on wine. I questioned whether he had drugged my drink... perhaps a slight poisoning. A mild arsenic. Belladonna. *Blue Of Noon* played itself out. Styn appeared concerned, yet amused by my predicament. Led me gently to his bed, began to bathe my face with a cool cloth. Suggested that perhaps the food was too rich, too sweet, spoiled. He began to flatter me, cooing how beautifully sickness suited me. How it created a lustrous pallor, a luminous sheen to my already pale skin. He claimed I was radiant, enthralling, a vision. It was making him hard. Erect. Would I mind if he simply released himself from his trousers, allowing his excitement some breathing room. He was choking in his pants. Murmuring all the while how sickness became me.

I begged him to assist me to the bathroom. I could no longer control the spasms racking my body. I needed to vomit, piss, shit. I was about to soil myself. He lovingly removed my dress, panties, bra, folding them neatly, and arranged them on the towel rack. His sophisticated manners reminding me of a well-paid man servant. He insisted I kneel at the toilet, purge myself, not be shy. He'd stay to help me. He hovered beside me, checking pulse, my temperature. The pupils of my eyes. The glare of the stark white tiles reflected off each other causing a vertiginous blur. My stomach heaved. I began to expel copious amounts of food, bile. Simultaneously pissing, shitting, all over the toilet, the tiles, my thighs. Racked with convulsions, my insides shooting out from every opening.

Passing in and out of consciousness. I lost track of time. Had no idea how long I lay crumpled beside the toilet. Shivering. My belly rumbling. The rapid fire machine gunning from the shutter of his camera startling me. The bastard had been photographing my entire seizure. Slowly I began to recover. Had the strength to raise my head, ask for a glass of water. Styn smiled sweetly, turning the shower on. Removing the huge goose-neck from the wall. Testing the temperature. He aimed it at the tiles above my head, a baptism of cool spray. He traced my outline on the floor, tickled my feet with pulsing jets, adjusting the nozzle, running the liquid massage up between my legs. Seductively upping the force. Holding it there just long enough for my pulse to race.

Then he hit my mouth. A cold hard fist of water, forcing lips apart, forcing me to swallow. Smiling as I began to choke. Shiver. He began to pull on his prick, which had remained exposed during the entire episode. Giving it a few strong pulls as he continued to focus the camera. Prodding my legs apart with the tip of his shoe. Planting a thick hose of water against my tiny blossom. My legs began a spastic thrash. My head pounding. Dry heaves ebbing. Orgasm mounting. The occasional flash bouncing off the white walls. I was too weak to protest. Vanity was useless. We both exploded. Burning this sickly vision into our collective memories like a short film for future recall.

He dropped the shower hose and knelt beside me. Kissing my feet. Murmuring in French, German, Dutch, litanies to my beauty. Gently washing me. An angelic smile kissing his lips. I was completely exhausted, paralyzed with fatigue. He carried me to his bed. Urging me to rest, sleep, gather my strength. Unable to protest the notes he was taking as the camera rewound.

"CHARLES MANSON IS IN MY HEART ALL WAYS..." was spray-painted in black two-foot high letters that ran the length of the abandoned hallway. I was still sore from battling the pitted streets of Hackney on the back of his Harley. "Smiffy" – makes him sound like a child's tattered teddy bear, but he looked like a greasy grizzly outlaw biker – smirked "Pritty, ain't it..." as he led me up to the third floor of a rancid squat.

Garbage littered the gangplank, stairwell, doorways, and even dangled from the bannister and light sockets. Discarded filthy remnants once worn as clothes steamed in piles. Mountains of leftover Kentucky Fried Chicken bones, mingled with fish and chip plastic takeaway plates which wrestled Curry To Go styrofoam and fought it out in the corners. The overall aroma, an intoxicating concoction of rotting flesh and excrément, escalated the nausea tap dancing up my oesophagus. "Home Sweet Home," the scruffy genius muttered. A man of few words. I spat up a spittle of vomit.

Smiffy had been recommended to me as a trusted "collector". If you were owed money, favours, or just wanted to fuck with someone's well being/paranoia, HE was the man to call. I had no urgent business requiring his services, but at 6ft 2" and 263 pounds I felt him a necessary addition to my loose-knit stable.

We left the bar on his bike stupidly shit-faced and ended up at his place miles outside of the city. All I wanted was a quick, cheap, dirty fuck. And the possibility of employing his unique talents sometime in the future. My patience was already exhausted by the time he kicked open the door to his room. "It only locks from the inside," was little consolation. I was sobering up quick.

I asked where the toilet was. He pointed at the corner. Asked if I wanted to use a t-shirt to wipe myself, but drip drying seemed more hygienic. I squatted facing him, slunk my tight black pants over my ass, around my knees, and pissed out the multiple vodkas I had consumed earlier. Right on the floor, a massive puddle swimming slowly toward his filthy mattress in the centre of the room. A long sigh caresses my lips, a small shudder ripples my flesh, and Smiffy stumbles over, drops to all fours and washes the last few trickles from my pussy. The smell of hot piss perfuming his pigsty. Alters the electricity in the atmosphere. The heat radiating outward warms the room by degrees. Charged particles perform an exotic ballet pirouetting off of dust motes.

His filthy tongue laps at my steamy mound like a hungry bear devouring a candy wrapper. He whips off his leather jacket, bathing huge hands and bulging biceps in the puddle of pissy liquor. Licking fingers and forearms, he offers me a taste. Dabbing my lips with two fat thumbs shoved roughly in my mouth. He sucks up a thick wad of mucus, phlegm and bile, spitting it deep inside my throat. I swallow it halfway down, allowing his juices to mingle with mine. Spit it right back at him. He pulls his prick free. Begins slapping it against the rough rotten piss-soaked floorboards. Pounding it mercilessly against the wood. Strangling the beast in a meaty fist, punishing the head. Pumping in grand agitation. Attempting to screw a hole in the floor. I suppress the laughter ping-ponging inside my belly. In a drunken stupor it doesn't matter what you fuck. As long as you're fucking something.

His grotesque moaning, the squelching of his fevered sex and the creaking wood, sound a song of diseased lust. The alcohol races through my blood, causing the room to spin. The vomit fermenting in my empty stomach launches itself upward, exploding from my mouth and nose. A small thick hot wad lands on his foreskin. In drunken delirium he explodes. His cum, the vomit and piss forging unholy matrimony in a fetid puddle at my feet. I laugh out loud as he rolls over, blows me a kiss and whispers "Ged night, Doll..." Passing out.

I clean myself up, walk to the corner and wait forty minutes for a car service to arrive. The morning sun bleeding slowly through the night sky. A grin twists my lips. I'll never see him again. Unless I need "collecting".

I had left Amsterdam a few days after my date with Styn. Took the night ferry to London. Called Murray, who I had met in Los Angeles. Offered if I ever needed a place to stay... I did.

He took me in. Hot road worker. As quiet as a cat burglar. Would leave for weeks at a time. Following the path of his own indiscretions. Kept our questions to ourselves. Open relationship. He loved torturing himself by sleeping on the couch, listening to me get fucked from the other room. Jerk off and dream. Leave early the next morning so as not to witness whatever it was I dragged out of bed. The only time I pissed him off was after an all nighter with a punk junkie rock singer who scrawled his name in blood on the bedroom wall. Used a crusty syringe as magic marker. Told Murray if he didn't appreciate the autograph to go and scrub it off with bleach. That blew his cool. Furious, he stormed out. Didn't matter. I had a date that afternoon with J.G.

I had been seeing J.G. for a couple of weeks. Set out to steal his vows of celibacy. I was turned on by his thousand yard stare, eyes that went on for miles. Reticence. His tortured genius wrestling libido. Decided to commit date rape. Fed him vodka and codeine to ease the pain. We soon became inseparable. Binge on Ecstasy. Trip over to his place on the fifteenth floor of a subsidized housing project in Brixton. Have hours of lushly orchestrated sex. A divine high, we'd cling to each other, fearful of slipping between the cracks in the floorboards. Dreamt we'd one day wake up to find ourselves melted like puddles, evaporated by the sun.

It was the first relationship I had where intimacy didn't equate with violation. I'm not sure J.G. felt the same way. I was still occasionally balling the road worker, a few of his friends and our mutual acquaintances. Which in itself wasn't as awful as my insatiable need to reveal in revolting detail the every nuance of my many indiscretions. It forced him into the voyeur's peephole. Whose microscopic magnification played itself out like a recurring nightmare. I adored him, yet it was impossible for me to curb my voracious philandering, sexual misanthropy, or gruesome revelations encapsulating the horrors inflicted upon my latest plaything, used and discarded like a broken toy whose warranty had expired.

Where all of my previous affairs had used creative energy to stimulate drama, we would construct drama by stimulating our creative energies. Both consumed with the art of self-flagellant confessionals, melodramatic operettas, musical Grand Guignol. Obsessed with creating gargantuan bodies of work which we would inflict upon the paying public. A variety of grotesque performances, the scope of whose horrific beauty is better left to the text books. We would tour Europe, Japan, the States, no spectator safe from the multi-tentacled lacerations that sprung from the hotbed of our philosophical sadomasochism.

The mobility we were afforded benefited our longevity. Stagnation the death of every relationship. While we travelled, caroused, performed, we shared a blissful co-existence. He was reserved, sensitive, introspective. I was obnoxious, arrogant, an exhibitionist. Polar opposites attracted to a higher middle ground.

London was beat. Back to New York with J.G. I'd been gone for four years. Returned to a crumpled city crucified beyond repair. A giant electro-magnetic force field feeding you false fuels. Agitates the nerve endings. Resulting in that chronic itch for more. And the more you get, the more you want. And more is never enough. Until it's too much. Until your life force feels like it's being continually sucked, milked, gnawed upon, ingested, digested and spat back at you by an army of living ghosts endlessly haunting a city whose borders are stretched to the point of utter insanity. And try keeping your sanity in New York. I dare you. The air itself is a psychotropic narcotic that accelerates the pulse rate.

And like any drug, you do too much, you feel filthied. Dirty. Rotting from the inside out. Never clean enough. Never free from the microbiotic flesh-eating bacteria. Never free from the botulisms, the staphylococcus, the airborne viruses, the tuberculosis, the sickness. No matter what lengths you go to to keep yourself clean. There is no safe distance once you've already been infected. A carrier full of diseased shrapnel. Sick to death of what passes for life. Sick of the stench of the living dead. The stench of urine, yeast and rotting corpses, both living and dead which assault the olfactories. Contaminated by small pools of viscous liquid which puddle in doorways, subways, sidewalks. Overhead pipes which leak a pus-like foul fluid tinged with toxic sludge and gasoline. Bathtubs, showers, sinks, rusted with the poisoned effort of a conduit no longer able to transport such noxious effluvium. I had already put in a five year stint in New York. I grew to despise it.

New York is a city that fears, yet embraces its own reflection. A gruesome portrait of decay, mortality, failure, fraud, whose caricatures are trapped inside a negatively charged environment whose collective scream is drowned out by the next drink, the next drug, the next lousy fuck.

The Arab shop boy from a Midtown shoe shop.

The Puerto Rican drug dealer from Spanish Harlem.

The black crack-head from Brooklyn.

The Egyptian magician moonlighting as a cab driver.

The Nicaraguan poet from the Lower East Side.

Crappy rock bands and their roadies.

The cruel Hasidics who preferred pinching to pussy.

Teenage virgins from New Jersey.

The hot blond sailer from Montreal who fucked me straight into the hospital after a three-day Ecstasy binge, his huge prick irresistible, awesome. Damaging.

One night stands that sometimes dragged on for weeks, months. I'd trip into someone else's daydreams, to suddenly wake up one morning and be done with them. Still living with J.G., who would listen patiently to a string of self-perpetuating obscenities, whose mounting horror he allowed me to catalogue, as if his was the analyst's couch. By the end of our relationship, he needed therapy. A retreat from my sickness. Pathological intoxication set in.

Alcoholism, insecurity complex, insanity. Addiction. And he still put up with me.

I knew I had to divorce myself from a city that offered up an endless influx of temporary distractions served up like junk food. Had to detox myself from the convulsive miasma of mindless activity whose goal may indeed be to over-stimulate, but whose resultant conclusion merely configures delusions of a grandeur that forever remains elusive. Bars, after-hours clubs, concerts, galleries, conversations which hoodwink your time and energy by convincing you of their urgency. The only pressing problem was waste removal. The need to cut out, cut off, all that conspires to distract.

Enter the Spanish Nazi.

He was born addicted to heroin on the 19th of March 1971 in the L.A. County Community Hospital. Conceived in hate, abuse began in the womb. Another unwanted, unwelcomed Latin loser. He came out screaming, contorted in pain. Twisted faces grimaced at the sight of another new-born junkie saddled with the sins of his father. Papa left Mama before the delivery hoping to score a dimebag, to celebrate the arrival, celebrate that the baby wasn't born deformed or brain dead, after all of Mama's beatings. Just a little bit fucked up.

Papa never returned after busting up his bike on the way back from East L.A. where the local Cholos insisted he join them in a toast to his first and only new-born son. Jack and smack didn't mix too well and Papa took a spill which wiped the shit-eating grin clear off his puss.

Mama didn't mind too much, blind to every need except the gnawing in her belly, the bruises between her skinny legs, and the unscratchable bitch of her addiction. She took the next shot on the delivery table twelve minutes after the prodigal son was shat out like a watermelon. Smuggled it in in the pocket of her housecoat.

His first meal was a weaning of methadone and

morphine, a failed attempt to quell the spasms racking through his bloated little belly. He kicked and cried and tried to wish himself dead in the cradle of the nursery surrounded by other undeserving unfortunates. All victims of boozy blood fucks, lust, ritual gang bangs. None, however, was less wanted than him. None more tempered with a vengeance to destroy a world that dared to condemn him to a life sentence under a rule of pain and hate. And never was there destined to become a more hate-filled fucker than him.

Black is the colour of my true love's hair. Creamy cocoa skin, the son of a devil's advocate grew up with a chip on his shoulder the size of Boulder Dam. At the age of four, he was beaten into his first coma by Mommy's latest lover. Back in the L.A. Community Hospital, he remained for three weeks as they traced the swelling and clotting. Hoping it wouldn't turn into permanent brain damage. The contusion suffered from the big black man's left hand left a delicate scar on his right eyebrow. That he lived was a shining testimonial to his predestined mission. A life-long tribunal littered with the scarring of the self-serving.

At six he played witness to the degenerate urges of a third generation coven of practising Devil worshippers. Passed from mouth to crack to cock, his mother initiated him into the Church of Satan. One of the many fuck toys brought into the delirious circle of the chronically demented. He was taught to please others and enjoy the natural desires he was too young to deny himself of. He quickly became an insatiable suitor in pursuit of his own pleasures. At the world-weary age of ten, he had already instigated an involvement with the next door neighbours, a family of eleven, who took turns taking out their multiple frustrations on his tender hide. Mother, grandmother, father, sons and daughters from six to sixty-two, beat at his bound and gagged body, calling out the names of saints and sinners alike. Like Christians at the altar of worship, they prodded, poked and pronged themselves into his willing flesh; cursing in the name of Satan and Salvation, they cleansed themselves of evil influence using him as a receptacle of their perverted restitutions. The weekly beatings went on for two years.

Born into a circle of fated pain, he learned first how to turn his hatred against himself and then against everyone else. By the age of twelve he had moved in with three other delinquents, themselves no strangers to cruelty. The Whoresome Foursome, as they came to be known around Hollywood, began practising and fine-honing their skills of verbal manipulations. Irresistible and charming, the teen terrors had the rules of the house spray-painted in Dayglo green near the front door. ONE FOR ALL AND FUCK YOU TOO. Filthy Swedish magazines littered the rancid squat, inspiring them on to new sexual horrors.

A string of teenage girls would wander in and out. The more often than not intoxicated young bait was usually blindfolded, beaten and raped by whoever was present at the time. Cigarettes seared inner thighs, bottles broke on kneecaps, fists and bricks did what they do best. Batter, bruise, bleed. Sex came as the final reward. The final insult. Here the young lords lacerated every opening with a vengeful deliverance. Tortures employed were waylaid upon the recipients who stood before them, reminiscent of the mothers they abhorred. They, like their fathers before them, harboured the disease of a sexual affliction whose credo was dominance.

After one particularly gruesome incident involving the genital scarification of a fifteen-year-old girl from the valley, the police force were summoned, thus ending their two-year long reign of terror at 452 Franklin Avenue. Since all the assailants were still under-age, no charges could be pressed. The cops simply destroyed the squat, sealed the lot it sat on, and sent the Whoresome Foursome packing.

At fourteen he was forced to return to his mother. Who by now couldn't stand the sight of him. Or the way his presence seemed to interfere with the endless flow of two-bit fuck-ups and assholes through the family home. She had a thing for alcoholic pill poppers, cast-offs from *Easy Rider*, *Dirty Harry*, *Street Car Named Desire*. Men that had suffered through long stretches at Sing Sing, Camirillo, San Quentin. The kind of men who didn't give a fuck how hard their lives had been as long as they could make someone else's life equally as miserable. And that usually meant him.

He started shooting dope with a gang of strung-out transvestites he befriended in the alleys and back streets of downtown L.A. Pimping and prostituting right alongside them. Collected twenty per cent off the girls' take for playing look out. Sixty percent when pulling three ways. Enough to keep up a one hundred and twenty five dollar a day habit. Which helped to deflect the pain from the endless beatings administered to him by the Peter Fonda lookalike who was shacked up with his mother. The third time 'Peter' tried to break his nose, he turned around and stabbed him twice in the chest screaming at the prick to "Hit me again and I'll fucking kill you..." It landed him in Juvie for two years. The judge didn't buy the self-defence plea.

Once incarcerated he learned the joys of self-mutilation. How by hurting yourself more than anyone else would ever want to, he could earn the respect of the other inmates. Always the first to fight, the hammering blows that pounded into him when outnumbered three to one could never match the viciousness that he would later reap upon himself. Alone in his bunk, the head bashing would begin. Smashing his head into damp cement walls, he tried to disappear the pain. Tried replacing an indescribable pain, somewhere in the base of his brain, with a concentrated self-inflicted throbbing. It somehow made the burden of his hatred easier to deal with. It was the same with the broken glass and rusty knifetips. It brought relief waiting for the scabs and bruises to slowly heal, knowing they eventually would. The psychic scars might not.

His mother always told him "Don't get mad... get even." So, on the afternoon of his release from Juvenile Detention he set her house on fire. Minor damage, she refused to press charges. Small admission of her own guilt.

He got strung out again. Hanging out at the sleazy bars near Hollywood and Vine. Picking up on aging Go-Go Girls, ex-strippers, prostitutes. Women used to his kind of abuse, mistook it for attention. Victims themselves, years lost to opiates, alcohol, addiction. Hook them on him. His own addiction to bone crushing power fucks. Twist them up inside until they'd love him just enough to support his various bad habits. Dust, speed, dope, coke cocktails.

Every sexual escapade became an act of unmitigated violence. Using any available icon, he punished ferociously the sins of his mother. Banging his full body weight into the willing receptors, blood would race from brain cells, fists become engorged. Pounding inside them, punching would follow. Black eyes, bruised lips, blood clots, teardrops. He took out on them what the rest of the world took out on him. His only satisfaction came through someone else's annihilation. To make them hurt as much as he did was the only way he knew how to relieve the pain he could no longer bear reliving.

It was a late autumn night after a serious session of titty

torture and humiliation involving Patty, a burnt-out thirty-three-year-old ex-Vegas showgirl fallen on hard times and bad luck, that he stumbled upon his mirror reflection. A beautiful teenage Latino girl sprawled out in the alley behind the showgirl's crash pad. Thinking her just drunk or fucked up he stumbled over kicking her in the ribs. Hard. No reply. Kicked her twice in the ass. Nothing. Cracked her head against the dumpster. No response. Slapped her soft velvety face. Again. Dead. Crumpled in a small wet heap. Steaming with piss and vomit. Stuck his hand in her pockets. Thirty bucks and an out of town I.D. She was fifteen. He took the needle from her inner elbow, tasting the blood crusted junk. Not bad. He lifted the tiny girl up over his shoulder, slipping her quietly into the trash receptacle. Making sure no one noticed. He travelled east, hoping to score a quick bag. Within minutes he was fixing a couple of alleys away, using the needle recovered from the human wreckage left rotting in the garbage. No sooner had the shit started rocketing into his bloodstream before the bile pushed upward pulsing into his throat and out of his mouth. "Not bad..." he grumbled before dropping to his knees. Crying. Heart-broken. He picked up the filthy needle, began plunging the spike over and over again into his arms, wrists, hands, neck. Stabbing wildly, searching frantically for a valve that would unhinge, release, set free. Trying to find that black hole, somewhere deep inside, that once plundered would concentrate all the pain, horror, heart-break into a solid-bodied centre. Looking for a way into the void that would lovingly engulf, lovingly embrace, lovingly surround, lovingly erase. Looking for somewhere, somehow, someone who could help him to house the unending cycle of pain and hate.

Looking for someone like me, who'd believe him whether he made it all up or not. Looking for a sister, mother, lover, fucker, white witch, goddess, wench, someone drenched in loving sympathy who could comfort him with unconditional understanding. Someone who KNEW. Someone who had been there before. Someone who could explain to him that there were no easy answers. No easy way out. No escape. From yourself. You had to LEARN to DEAL with the cards you were dealt. Had to learn the hard way that the world doesn't OWE you a fucking thing. Not a reason, nor excuse. No apologies. Had to learn that some forms of insanity run in the family, pure genetics, polluted lifelines, full of disease. Profanity. Addiction. Co-addiction. Inability to deal with reality, what the fuck ever that's supposed to mean when you're born into an emotional ghetto of endless abuse. Where the only way out is in... deep, deep inside, so you poke holes in your skin, thinking that if you could just concentrate the pain it wouldn't remain an all-consuming surround which suffocates you from the first breath of day to your last dying day. Day in. Day out. Day in and out. I knew all about it.

He'd been clean for eight months. Met him at a small party. First reaction was to smack him in the fucking face. Something about him crawled under my skin. Immediately. He walked in with Jennifer, a friend of a friend. She took me aside and asked me to take him off her hands. Wanted to just unload him, couldn't deal with his bullshit any more. He was beautiful but fucked up. Sober, but full of shit. A pathological liar, petty thief, non-stop hustler. His smile could charm the panties off of you. She told me to beware, but thought I might be able to straighten him out. I was still trying to straighten myself out.

He bothered me so much it made me curious. You'd think I'd be able to recognize a soul-sucking predator. Being one myself. Maybe that was the attraction. The challenge.

Lydia Lunch

Like any charlatan he was charismatic. Magnetic. He glowed. His force-field irresistible. His smile decimating. He seemed so incredibly happy. His hook.

I was warned about him by everyone who knew him. I ignored it. Thought I could make it different. Feed him the understanding, knowledge, wisdom to drop the victim turned victimizer guise. Even though I was still working on it myself. Still working on it.

He followed me out to San Francisco. Unloaded his life story on the front porch of the local Acid Guru. A brilliant Argentinian professor who I was staying with. Specialized in collecting memorabilia from Leary, Kesey, Liddy, the Haight. Offered us his pad for the weekend. Took off for Big Sur. Asked politely that we not set the bed on fire. The quilt once belonged to Janis Joplin.

My latest flame's magnetic charm soured suddenly during foreplay. Once a junkie, always a junkie. Hooked on drama. Like myself. The sex was a brutal test of physical endurance. Both of us battering the other into submission, neither one of us wanting to be the first to throw in the bloody towel. We passed out for a few hours. Woke up and started right back in. The sex ugly, vicious, hot.

We spent the weekend in bed. His stint with the Church of Satan recollected through sex magick, hypnosis, past life regression. Brought me back to a place in time I had frequented often in dreams, fantasy. Assumed his role of Spanish Nazi Dictator during the bloodthirsty Inquisition. I played arrogant Heretic chained to the master's chamber. A willing victim of murderous pathology. Blind. Bound. Gagged. Hogtied. Sliced up, strung out in a time zone Past/Present/Future/not wanting to return to the here and now, but be forever lost, trapped inside a haunted limbo, a sexual vertigo. Entombed in a self-obsessed sarcophagus of torture. His torture. My torture. Hundreds of years of endless collective torture role-played out again and again.

I should have known better. In truth I did. I had been warned. But I knew exactly what I was doing. I always knew what I was doing. I just didn't stop myself. I never stopped myself. Especially when I knew better.

To escape from the extreme psychic pollution shrouding New York, I ran off to New Orleans. Whose culture of psychic extremes has been cultivated for hundreds of years under the guise of Voodoo, Hoodoo, Santeria, Black Magic, Creole folklore and congenital Vampirism. Atmospheric toxins contribute to a geographical sickness plaguing the city whose seat lies three feet below sea level. Its mouth a gaping maw suckling the muddy sludge off the banks of the filthy Mississippi.

I was drawn to New Orleans' decaying beauty, ripe with overgrown vegetation which both blossomed and rotted in the very same breath. Swooned by the intoxicating delicacy of lush gardenias, night blooming jasmine, and sweet olive trees whose healing aromas and heavenly perfume would subdue even the sourest dispositions. Then, as suddenly as one turns a corner, the olfactories are assaulted by clouds of noxious fumes boiling over the flimsy man-hole covers used as trashcan lids for the underground garbage receptacles. Which offer no protection from the gruesome stew of dead fish, bell peppers, and dirty baby diapers left decomposing in the still afternoon swelter, its stagnant humidity and oppressive heatwaves conspiring to produce fainting spells, narcolepsy and shortness of breath.

I was spellbound by the decadent architecture, the elaborate sprinkling of wrought iron balconies. Sweeping porches flanked by floor to ceiling windows, darkened with wooden shutters to help beat back the mid-day sun. Backyards full of weeping willows whose droopy arms would form plump tents canvassing the trees.

My only contact in New Orleans was Bettina, a sexy German ex-patriot on business leave from a career as chanteuse of a post-industrial cabaret act who specialized in stealing haunted melodies out of Dietrich's scrap-book. Bettina, bored with the laboured machinations of the music industry, became an investment banker. Was managing a dilapidated mansion situated on the edge of the French Quarter, which she bought at a city auction. She petitioned to have it granted historical status, was renovating and planning to sell back to the city. At a two hundred per cent profit margin. In the meantime it had been vacant for almost a decade; they'd already cleaned the place out, I was welcome to play house sitter until I landed an apartment.

A few days after my arrival a man lay dead six blocks from the front door of the mansion on Gov. Nicols. Bettina and I were returning from coffee. We gunned it in under a red light on the corner of Esplanade. An elderly black man, stepping off the crosswalk was too entranced by my flaming red hair and too-tight white t-shirt, to notice the donut delivery truck barrelling at him from the other direction. He was thrown thirty feet straight up in the air and landed with a skull-splitting shudder in the middle of the street. Welcome to the Big Easy.

I rented a small house whose backyard bordered a convent. Morning coffee was taken on the huge screened-in back porch, whose view afforded me the daily spectacle of nuns frolicking, often engaged in vicious games of volleyball or badminton. My next door neighbour was a teenage queen with borderline personality disorder and musical aspirations of attending Juilliard. Until then, every Sunday found him banging out hymns at a local Baptist church. I left New York, sick of being crowded, hassled, harassed, hounded and oogled to reside beside a flaming peeping tom whose rampant voyeurism would often lead him directly to my bedroom window. A blank stare, frozen smile, flippant demeanour. There was nothing I could do to discourage him. One afternoon he telephoned to invite me to lunch. I sarcastically replied, not today, I was busy, engaged in a naked ritual communing with the devil. He interrupted to correct me. He could see me sitting in a sundress, fully made up, my legs crossed, daintily bouncing my left foot up and down. He was watching me through a small crack between curtain and shade, standing on my front porch, cordless phone in hand. I screamed at him to go home. And stop his obsessive spying. Of course, he wouldn't.

I assumed relocating to New Orleans would offer up a fresh start. I had removed myself from everyone I knew, wanted to settle into a comfortable numbness and recuperate from the previous thirty years. That lasted about a month. I got a call from the Spanish Nazi, inviting himself down for a short visit, bored with L.A., or more likely, neck deep in bullshit from spinning one too many lies to the wrong party. I foolishly relented. He showed up two days later. And stayed for three weeks. By the end of which I was ready to kill him. Sure he had come to kill me.

Demented fantasies of him being ordered down from high ranking officials in The Church of Satan, who had elected me a ritual victim worthy of sacrifice. What better location than Death's Other Kingdom, where the electricity of magic is forever illuminating the doorways that lead to the next dimension.

I was originally attracted to the Spanish bastard, under the misguided impression that through therapy and recovery, he had miraculously been transformed from battered child out to avenge the world, to mischievous imp ready to forgive, forget and get on with it. So smooth was his ruse. I was hoodwinked.

His glee, an effervescence whose sparkle could anaesthetize, was regrettably endlessly overshadowed by deep depression, black moods, temper tantrums the scope of which could darken an entire city block. There was no crawling out from under such a spectre. Like a torrential spring downpour, one could only pray that it would soon pass.

We'd spend days transfixed in sexual delirium, his cheap parlour tricks effective enough to delude me into believing he was indeed the Prince of Darkness he mirrored his image upon. I should have known better. Master of schemes, scams, rip off. A beautiful package. Unfortunately, he was full of shit.

Had probably lied to me about everything. I didn't even know his age. He'd given me at least three different interpretations of every story that left his lips. I, myself was prone to weaving fanciful yarns spun like fairy tales of mysterious origins, but still maintained the capacity to inject enough realism to steer the punchline toward fact, not fantasy. He had somehow lost the ability to differentiate. When trapped in a web of his own fiction, he'd turn defensive, lash out. It became stifling, intolerable. I sent him away.

He continued to stalk me. Hour-long phone calls, begging apologies. When I refused him re-entry into my life, my house was bombarded with electrical discharges, which would send cupboards and closet doors banging open and closed like a spastic child having a seizure. Rooms would be flooded with negatively charged atoms producing a force field impossible to navigate through. An exorcism was in order.

Holy water, salt, sage. An effigy of the bastard who I had imagined had been pursuing me through multiple lifetimes. An attempt to remove the burden of his curse, whose weight was a heavy cross made unbearable by his belief that I was born to shoulder it.

I rebounded by having an affair with a beautiful teenage manchild. I was cycling toward the park one day, trying to untangle myself from the Spanish Nazi's long distance tentacles. He was still phoning. Still stalking. Still obsessing. It was awful. Suddenly a lanky vision, dressed in black, sped past me in the opposite direction, legs and arms akimbo, towering over a ratty bicycle's rusty frame. My nipples responded. I vacantly pinched one. I wanted to call out, to follow him. Kicked myself for not trusting my instinct. On arriving home, I ran into the queen from next door. Commiserated over returning empty-handed, disappointed for having let slip such a tasty morsel. The queen probed, begging me to relive the details. Where did I spot him. What make of bike. Blue or brown eyes. Black, blond or brunette hair. Boots, shoes or sneakers. Turning conspiratorial, he insisted he could set up a date for the following night. Eddy lived only a few blocks away. The queen had been offering him blowjobs for months. At least now he'd be able to have a ringside seat, no doubt outside my bedroom window, to witness the deflowering.

The next morning my backyard was resplendent with quaint wrought iron tables and chairs pilfered from a local café or wealthy neighbour. A small handwritten note read "purloined for your pleasure... at your service... Edward

Rex..." Fuck flowers, Eddy was courting me with furniture. That it was stolen made it even more precious.

He arrived promptly at nine. Regaled in knee-high storm troopers, black button-down shirt, red arm band, raging erection. A fetishist's wet dream. A well mannered, highly evolved, self-styled Hitler Youth. Seventeen years old. He'd live with me for a year and a half, making the occasional trip back to his parents' to retrieve books, clothes, his twelve-year-old brother.

We shared an interest in the secret life of inanimate objects. Constantly foraging for rusty implements, fascinated with rebirth, decay, regeneration. Construct small pouches of potent gris-gris, which we'd fill with powerful herbs, white birch, cicada wings, teeth, small bones. A white witchcraft configured around the purity of youthful intuition. My vampirism returning to suckle on the sun's (son's) blood.

It was heavenly spending time with someone whose limited life experience had spared him the endless cycle of affair, anger, entropy, recovery, relationship, affair, anger, entropy etc... which I, just like everyone I know, have suffered from.

And I, far from perverting the tender blossom of his youth, allowed him the freedom to fully express his natural tendencies. Encouraged him to explore his every desire. Make real his fantasies. I would tie him to the bed, handcuff him to the bars on the bedroom window. Sitting upright in a kitchen chair. Bound and blindfolded. Leave the house for an hour or two. Allow his mind to wander. Fantasies to overwhelm. Return to the musky scent of his orgasm, still warm, wet. Teenage lust ripe in the air. Free him from his self-satisfied bondage. Take him roughly. Squirting all over him. Pounding him off. Until light-headed, we'd collapse. Infants at nap.

But bliss is short-lived when one prefers to sup on

melodrama. I had been pleasantly numb for months. Was starting to get itchy. Eddy and I were ready to move on, both felt our relationship had reached a glorious peak and to continue would only produce stagnation.

I was offered a short teaching stint, one semester at the San Francisco Art Institute. Invited to take over the Performance/Video department. Run it as I saw fit. A paid vacation, hired to experiment in mind control, group hypnosis. I took it on a lark. Pulled once more in a westerly direction. What could be easier than taking twenty students, weaning them off their idealistic trust-fund lollipops, renouncing their theories of art grants and giving them a dose of hardcore reality. The theme of my class was fearlessness, how to create without a budget and the importance of autobiographical bloodletting elevated to a new art form.

It wasn't long before vicious rumours circulated throughout the school. Of course I insisted my students encourage gossip. Spread little white lies about how we had formed a coven rife with Black Magic, Devil worship, ritual sacrifice. Orgies. Outlandish exaggerations, or merely an insight into the inner workings of a twisted Head Mistress who knowingly cultivated the abuse of power. The line was very fine, indeed.

I began an affair with one of my students. A tortured Italian graffiti artist whose tag read SICK. He'd slink into class dressed in trenchcoat and stocking cap. Screwdriver in right pocket. Steel toed boots. Questioning whether it had been me who was psychically stalking his Oakland loft, encouraging late night sessions of mind-blowing masturbation. My spectral aura hovering over his bed. Urging him on. In my direction.

I admitted having been summoned to San Francisco.

Knew something, someone was waiting. Had spent weeks prior to my departure with my mind's eye wandering an astral roadmap through train tracks, back streets, bedrooms, alleys. A blind search for the source of what was calling. I knew it was him.

I was installed in a Mission apartment, compliments of the school, strangely enough a few blocks from my first liaison with the Spanish Nazi. Who still continued to plague. I had invited Bart over under the premise of reviewing a piece he had performed for the class. A monologue detailing the struggle of deprogramming one's self from the clutches of organized religion after having been brain-washed by their brilliant bullshit for four years.

I was intrigued by the concept of translating the knowledge and worship of Divine Love into layman's terms. Applying Love of God into Love of Goddess. Casting myself in the starring role. Infatuated with the vision of one so selfless that he would willingly put his life on hold as he travelled door to door preaching the gospel. He had spent two years as a missionary. Was still in the process of extricating himself from religion's morbid deathgrip.

I offered to give Bart a healing. An alchemist's ritual of using positive energy to purge the negative ions surrounding his body's force field. A ten-foot shield riddled with suspicion, paranoia, doubt. A health mistrust which accompanied his recovery from the ministry's stranglehold.

The 'psychic' invites the 'recipient' to relax. Drawing in deep breaths allowing the mind to neutralize, drift. Empty. With a calculated series of hand gestures, one circulates the blocked energy, clearing a pathway for the chakras to open. When done correctly, euphoria usually follows. But it's an unpredictable science at best. The last time I had been the beneficiary, I was sent spinning into a previous incarnation, twisted nightmare. Forced to witness my own vivisection. At the hands of a madman reminiscent of the Spanish Nazi. A technicolour bloodbath as real as it was hundreds of years before.

Bart sat on the edge of the bed. I began to manipulate the atmosphere. Scattering energy to the four corners. Stimulating air flow. The room began to expand. Its dimensions doubling, tripling. Quadrupling. We had blown a hole through a doorway into another realm. The walls turned a sickly grey nimbus lined with slippery entities whose evil demeanours undulated, taunted. I felt possessed by the torture ghosts of beings both living and dead, who were seeking a vehicle through which they could translate their ungodly anguish.

An orgy of ectoplasmic slugs began forcing themselves out of Bart's mouth. Scattering to the edges of the room. Swelling in size and number. A hideous vision that both repulsed and amazed. A corrupt intermingling of Voodoo, Black Magic and Exorcism. The entire room bathed in cloudy shadows. A milky fog. We collapsed, petrified, clinging to each other in desperation. Fearful of being sucked into the vortex, that sewer of lost souls whose polluted origins were impossible to decipher. An endless Limbo unfolding before us.

I ran to open the window. Fresh air to disperse atmospheric sludge. Demagnetize the electricity. A cool breath of salt current slices through the pus. Which puddles out into the street. Whose empty silence is shattered by a single gunshot boomeranging off the wet sidewalk. We duck for cover. A squad car's siren follows within seconds. The block gets a lock down. Bookended in black and white. A merry-go-round of red lights. Our sickness a contagion.

We spent the weekend consumed in sexual nirvana. Surrendering to the freedom of censoring from our psyche all but the most voluptuous sensations. An otherworldly union which opened celestial gateways through which we disappeared for days. Impossible to return to clock time while still bathed in efflorescent light, healing from a psychic purge.

The semester was over. I was returning to New Orleans. Hesitant to leave Bart behind. But I was still living with Eddy. I'd have to ask him to leave. Plan my next move.

Bart called me a week later. Had dropped out of school, quit his day job and was locked out of his loft by his roommate. A beefy Latin sculptor who smoked enough pot to realize that if you dabble in magic, even subconsciously, you risk losing your mind. Which he assumed Bart had. Convinced he would end up institutionalized. Incarcerated. Fearful for him, of him, fearful of the spell we had cast. So he kicked Bart out. Who by now was suffering from delusions of grandeur, chemical imbalance, hypoglycaemia, borderline schizophrenia, and multiple personality disorders. Neuro-chemical transmitters overloaded by the electricity in the atmosphere. San Francisco nearly vibrates with electrical disturbances. Another city whose geographical peculiarities rifle the atmosphere. Disequilibrium shatters the sensitive soul.

Bart was forced out into the street. A self-appointed martyr with a Christ Complex turned Urban Shaman. Where once he walked the streets preaching to others the path to locating the gods within themselves, he was now reduced to co-habitating with the godlessness and ever-present evil loitering on every street corner in any city whose sidewalks and doorways are your only shelter. His only protection, the screwdriver in his trenchcoat's pocket. I sent him a ticket to New Orleans. Death's Other Kingdom. Insane with anticipation.

The moment he stepped inside my living room, the

portals once more expanded, our combined chemistry lit the room with diffused light whose amber rainbow puddled in corners. We celebrated our reunion with hours of glorious fucking. His prison sentence of celibacy, which had lasted for four years under the ministry's meddling eye, forever commuted. As a lover he was madman, twisted minister, devout follower, expert conjurer. Wrapped inside the teenage body of a demented artist poisoned on aerosol fumes. An intoxicating combination.

Time would evaporate. Days melted into each other. New Orleans' endless summer alchemy, a magician's delight. Travelling both backward and forward in time, the psychic landscape a battlefield where wars once waged would rage again. Revisiting multiple lifetimes whose victories and sorrows were ours to relive. Heavenly torture.

Our psychosis had escalated. Illuminations would manifest off of inanimate possessions. Haunted by history's insistence on repetition. Visions emanating in furious succession. We were both losing it. Bart questioning if I was spiking the food. Feeding him acid, mescaline, mushrooms, cyanide. I confided I would often flavour meals with my body's juices. Blood, urine, mucus, secretions. Old Cajun recipe. You could train a dog by feeding it your sweat. Worked just as well on humans. Practised by many a seductress. I doubted it was causing hallucinations.

We were trapped in a Voodoo of our own design. Fucking four, five, six times a day. Too hot to sleep. Too wired to eat. Dehydrated. Our bodies, dirty little puppets, whose master would not reveal himself, preferring instead to entangle us in a mystical hotbed of lust, dementia, madness. Forced to do battle against ourselves, each other, and the multiple others who were fighting for dominance and possession of our powers. To reason.

Both of us rippling through hundreds of

personalities, as if the remote control had crashed, flipping from one channel to the next, occasionally stalling over the renunciations put forth by an ex-member of the clergy who had spun 360 degrees many times over and had returned to the pulpit to once more deliver yet another speech which would fall upon deaf ears. Bart attempted to warn me, I was too stubborn to listen. We were both insane.

An all-day battlecade. My vehement denials the target. Windows were shattered. Books burned. Photos destroyed. Dressers and desks tipped on their side, spilling their orphaned contents in sad little piles, the tattered remnants bruised by an unholy home invasion. The enemy within let loose to rampage. Neither safe from ourselves, nor each other. A brutal exorcism inflamed our madness.

The police were summoned. I contemplated shooting both of us before they arrived. At thirty-three I was suffering from my own Christ Complex. Convinced that this was the culmination of my sordid Death Trip. I was sure it was my time to go. It was. To Charity Hospital Psychiatric Ward. To check Bart in. Before we killed each other. He was under the delusion that our entire misadventure was an elaborate performance piece, staged without script, being video taped and docu-drama'd as a televised event simulcast over the airwaves. It should have been. The opening credits, a schizoid graffiti scrawl... The Animals moaning "There is a house in New Orleans..."

The cops escorted us into the reception area. Full of alcoholics, drug addicts, manic depressives, the parents of acid casualties. Old men and women with nowhere else to go. Hoping to escape the afternoon's swelter.

New Orleans by nature is a swamp whose gases ebb forth from the murky pools of stagnant water encircling its perimeter. Humidity expands the gas trapping its poison close to the surface. Rotting vegetation emits fumes of carbon dioxide. Electricity runs through the centre of the city, powering trolley cars which transport stale souls housed in bodies poisoned from over-rich food, pollution and bad genetics. Over- and underground cables form a barrier shield which prevents negative energy from escaping the boundaries of its primordial polarity. It is a breeding ground for illness, virus, sickness, self-destruction and insanity.

Bart had never looked more beautiful. Hand-cuffed behind his back, dirty bare feet, low-slung Levis, and a bare chest, chicken-dancing around the lobby, making small talk with the other outpatients, who all appeared desperate to bum a cigarette, get their medication refilled or insist that they were only there on a visit.

I filled out the forms for his admission. He assumed I was checking us both in. I probably should have. They brought us up to the ward for evaluation. First strapping him into an ancient wheelchair whose rusty tires squealed and wheezed. The ante-room stale with dead air, sour breath, body odour. Crowded with inmates whose delirium tumbled forth in fits and starts. Hysterical laughter followed by alligator tears. Rambling monologues quoting Shakespearian rhapsodies. Spates of uncomfortable silence. Facial tics. Vulgar gestures. Obscenities.

I knew I had to get him out of there. But once you entered the ward, a pass was needed to appease the armed guard who kept watch outside the locked steel door. We were summoned into the doctor's office. Scaly and reptilian, as twisted as any of his patients. Apologized that an evaluation could not be performed until Monday. Two days away. He was finishing up his rounds, didn't have the time to squeeze us in. Suggested Bart relax at the hospital until then. Panic set in.

I shut the door to his office. Barricading the three of

us in. Urged the doctor to listen to me. I had made a mistake. What I had mis-diagnosed as madness, loss of self-control, schizophrenia, was merely exhaustion. Malnutrition. An allergic reaction. Stress. Explained how Bart's childhood had been haunted by both human and otherworldly hellraisers who had plagued an only son's lonely nights. Forced into solitaire while his single mother moonlighted on the graveyard shift; many midnights would come and go to find him intoxicated with fear, searching for the source of hushed whispers, sudden flashes of light, the tapping on the glass. And now, sent forth on a whim, landing in a strange city, he was unable to derail the morbid vertigo which trails childhood's brutal memories. Memories that had only recently begun to surface. Hoping that illumination would put an end to his paralysing fear of abandonment. His hatred of other men, both his horrible father, as well as Daddy's replacements, his rebellion against authority. Coupled with having been homeless, thrown out into the street by his best friend, forced to walk for days on end, unsure of his next meal, afraid to rest, fearful of being made victim in his sleep. All he needed was rest. Food. Water. To recover. Promising that if the doctor would be so kind as to allow me to check him out, I'd assume full responsibility for his well-being. The doctor, too tired to argue and unable to outsmart me, reluctantly let us go. We ran to the exit. Delirious.

Years lost in vicious accusations, bitter curses, myopic monologues. Followed by infernal silence. Thick, sour air hanging like a noose dangling obscenely. Blood rush consumes reason. Dislocation follows. A hollow forms. The vortex swallows. It is absolutely impossible to talk sense into me under such conditions.

Time after time, with one man after another, I would find myself engaged in endless conversations, practising the art of spinning circles around them. No doubt, in part, due to my stubborn inability to admit anything other than the most incriminating. Few men actually want as much revealed. And I'll admit EVERYTHING. Except that I'm wrong. Except that I'm guilty. I'm sure I've been wrong on any number of things, in many given circumstances. But I'd never admit it. Ever. I don't remember ever FEELING guilty. EVER. But I'm sure I am. Of just about everything.

I've never lost a single argument. I wouldn't admit it even if I had.

I've been called insane, a sociopath, out-of-my-fucking-mind, a lunatic, deranged, demented, heartless, a bitch, cunt, slut, whore, manic-schizophrenic paranoid... an evil, cold, calculating, controlling alien-robot. All by people who loved me or said they did or thought they did. Although they probably didn't ever really know me. Didn't know the REAL me. Knew only what I'd let them know. Knew only so much.

I was very open, loving, responsive, supportive, giving, generous. When I wasn't a deranged, schizophrenic, sociopathic heartless cunt, possessed with an incredible ability to fluctuate wildly at any given time under many given circumstances.

So good was I at compartmentalizing every aspect of my life, that there were huge sections of myself, that even I would lose sight of. Massive sweeps of memory would disappear. Chunks, blocks, years of time would evaporate. As if nothing before that very moment had existed as far back as I could recall. As if life and death hung suspended between the four walls around me now. Time fell away and with it every day of the last thirty years was erased. I could remember a backwash of history, but not my own.

My moods could swing violently between breaths, lasting a few moments or for years. At times each new sentence, every syllable would sing a separate song filled with dissonant melodies and fractured harmonies. A single word could trigger a chain reaction in the right brain which would catapult my opponent, partner, lover, fucker, into a contrary conversation with a distant relative of whoever it is they perceived me to be.

Often in that split second of a mood shift, I would forever lose interest in the passive victim who had prodded the arrival of another disparate personality. Of course I would seek out men who themselves, were victims of radical adrenal overload, manic fluctuations, chemical imbalance, wild mood swings. This game became a dance of two fighters shadow boxing. Each trying desperately to survive not only the self, in its multiple fractures, but to overcome, dominate, and triumph over the deadly opponent who spits back with equal venom the poisoned rantings of an equally disturbed psyche.

A vampirism I was adamant to admit to, even when exposed to the dying remains of my latest kill.

I started to get frightened of my own libido. My sexual urgings, ravenous desires, a beast forever banging on the door. Continuing to seek out nameless, faceless strangers. Hoping to find one, ten, a hundred who could quell this sickening hunger, quench an unbearable thirst. Who could abate this exhausting search for other, another, more.

I was a sexual predator, consumed by the need to feed. To feed in. To find someone, anyone, something, anything, that could feed into me what I needed. The need became an impossible irritant. I was looking to possess, to consume, what they possessed that most reminded me of myself. That most reminded me of an inextinguishable luminescence, that radar of a dead star whose ghost shall never cease to cast shadows. I was looking in vain for myself as I willingly disappeared inside of others.

Of course to fill the void within, only the self will suffice. We reach this realization only after we've stuffed every hole, every orifice, every opening with an indiscriminate array of pointless junk. Wreckage. Waste. Human offal. And still hunger remains unsatisfied, especially when the object of desire is forever in flux. Gluttony is never satisfied, whether it's for sex, food, or drugs. It begs to be fed an enormous amount of useless stimulation, information, trivial soundbites, random affections, unrelated facts and figures. Forgettable fucks.

And the more you've had... the more you want. An endless cycle of multiple frustrations. Where nothing seems to satisfy. Not even in dreams.

And my dreams were full of blistering hallucinations on an epileptic scale. A crash of limbs and legs, crusty with the browning blood of a transgenerational orgy. Where hundreds of bodies flail wildly in slow motion like a bad acid flashback marrying Bosch to Bundy. Bruises and scars rippling like varicose veins under black light. The returning ghosts of all those I had sexed began re-emerging like a flash flood bursting the memory banks.

History, reduced to thousands of snapshots rifled through the air like a broken film-strip ripped through an ancient projector forcing the mind to work in multiples, tripping over images begging for recognition. Begging for deliverance from the place where time smoulders.

I longed to escape the perimeter of this fleshy prison, to disappear into milky nimbus, blurry-eyed, light-headed. Longed for a permanent amnesia, a catatonia which forgoes responsibility, the enemy of freedom. Wanted to erase dreams, memory, vision, to ultimately forget every word, every face, every nightmare. But I couldn't. I can't forget. I remember too much. Remember every detail, nuance, am forced to repeat even the most repellent occurrence. My sanity insists upon it. Insists upon expulsion. Purgation. Insists I wring from every cell, the poisoned thoughts, polluted deeds, malicious intentions, that would, if not puked forth, riddle me with disease. Sickness. Death.

And I feared that Death picks up where life left off. An endless barrage of unbearable obstacles. A god-forsaken terrain where lost souls find even less mercy. A shattered dreamstate where every somnambulant second is plagued by the nightmarish preoccupation of one's own fears. A bleak panorama where not even Death offers any release, for what you wrought will come back to haunt. As if the struggle never ends. As if there is not now, nor ever has been peace. Peace being foreign to my nature. The nature of the fucking beast.

I feared the repercussions of hundreds of thousands of lifetimes sweeping through a sea of history, threatening to drown me. I was married to the invisible anniversaries which celebrated the accumulation of everything I was, of everyone I had known. Of everyone I had been. And it still wasn't enough. I felt somehow removed from my own experiences, as they washed over me, blurring the interpretation between reality and fantasy. Past and present. My life and the thousands of others I had consumed both in daydreams and nightmares.

I had to de-program myself. From myself. Had to re-invent rituals of purification. So full of the vagrant pollutions of others. It was time to de-tox. Not only from alcohol, sex and drugs, but from the needy leeches who looked to me to swab their sores. De-tox from my own needy lechery. Had to locate the centre wound and cauterize. Undo the original sin, the origin of my sickness.

Had to learn to replace Them, It, Want, Hurt, Anger, Sorrow, Loss, with Power, Healing, Wisdom, Fulfilment, Satisfaction.

I decided to lock myself in. A forced segregation. Sabbatical. A retreat into myself. My selves. Play hide and go seek in the looking-glass. The mirror angled at the foot of my bed. Twisted reflections bouncing off into infinity. Obsessed with my image, the myriad of distorted figurines who danced in front of me in rapid succession, every feature exaggerated, every slight imperfection a new delicacy. Glorious wonder at the body's capacity for renewal. Regeneration. Every self-induced orgasm an exercise in life extension. My narcissism unbound, marvelling in delight at the sculpture of the female form.

I began to realize exactly how much of my energy

I had been squandering on other people. On men. Men who would never understand that I would always want more than they were ever capable of giving. More than what was even fair to demand. More than they would ever be able to give, even if they knew how. Because I didn't need them. I needed myself. To reclaim myself. To reclaim my capacity for pleasure. I was simply using men to stimulate myself. To stimulate that necessary adrenal rush, that ultimate kick, that heavenly high, that blinding white light that accompanies every orgasm. Those extra-celestial explosions which cascade in ripples, reminding you that you are truly, truly alive.

And that surely you must also die. And is Death not the ultimate orgasm, a return to that other-worldly ether, whose very origins were indeed a Big Bang, the ultimate explosion, the supreme chaos, whose resonance is the vibration we constantly seek to reproduce in everything we do. In every breath we take. In every orgasm. Faked or not.

I was always vain. My vanity saved me. Kept me sane. Kept me from falling overboard. I suffered from extremes of passion, insatiability, gluttony. But I always knew when to pull away. Pull out. Knew how far I could go before being swallowed, before sinking into the pitfall of self-loathing, addiction, depression.

I was surrounded by manic depressives who battered themselves with the nearest available weapon. Vodka, scotch, beer, coke, dope, pot, pills, poppers, uppers, downers, in-betweeners. All of which I too indulged in. None of which I ever gave myself over to. None of which ever applied the stranglehold.

I have lived surrounded by entire communities drunk on oblivion. Drunk on Death. Drunk to avoid the nauseating confrontation that pits the user against that which they abuse. I was drunk on fuck. Drunk on the charged electricity coursing through the vortex between muscle and bone, expanding inches, feet, miles beyond the skin. Stimulating an itch in inner space. I was strung out on the elevation of blood pressure, the escalation of heart rate. Shallow breaths which starve the brain of oxygen. Suffocation. Hooked to an extraneous power source which I bled like a cipher from the souls of unsuspecting victims.

about the author

To be, the saying goes, is to be cornered. From the off Lydia Lunch came out fighting. All her acts – she has always had the good grace to hesitate to call them art, though from the outside her claims are greater than many – have been about clawing back the space to call her own. Be it music, film-making, spoken word performance, writing, photography or body sculpture, her work is characterised by a need to penetrate to the core of her subject to unearth some truth, which she then unhesitatingly articulates, no matter how ugly or damaging it may appear. Because she deals with what she knows best, that is, herself and her full-on impact on the world, her revelations are pitched as *Incriminating Evidence*, to quote the title of her 1992 collection of performance pieces (published by Last Gasp). But if she pleads guilty to everything it is neither from remorse nor out of some catholic urge for redemption. Rather, it is out of acknowledgement of her insatiability, born of abuse, for experience parlayed through music, word, artwork into cathartic expression that might put her on speaking terms with her demons. For all of this would be as nothing if she could not find the means to make sense of her experiences. As her third book *Paradoxia* documents, the desire for expression drove Lunch, born 1959, to New York from upstate. Then aged 14, she had little to sustain her except anger and wit. In the late 1970s she played guitar and sang in Teenage Jesus & The Jerks, the influential No Wave group she formed with James Chance. As Lydia's first declaration of hostile intent, Teenage Jesus laid out the gospel she would thereafter remain true to – when Lydia says "No", she means it, and once said, that's it. Her other music activities include the groups Eight-Eyed Spy and 13.13, her alternative doomed cabaret singer persona "Queen Of Siam", plus collaborations with The Birthday Party, Jim Thirlwell and Rowland S Howard. She has also written and acted in various films and Off-Off Broadway theatre productions. The two movies she scripted and performed for director Richard Kern – **The Right Side Of My Brain** and **Fingered** – are now acknowledged as underground classics.

In the early 1980s she began stripping the music away to leave the words standing naked. With the spoken word cassette, *The Uncensored Lydia Lunch*, released through her own Widowspeak Productions, set up to look after her various projects, Lunch pioneered a new form of confrontational performance. Numerous music and spoken word releases followed, including a collaboration with Hubert Selby Jr, Henry Rollins and Don Bajema. Her strangest "literary" project took place in 1988, when she formed the hardcore trio Harry Crews with Sonic Youth's Kim Gordon, by way of tribute to the then undersung Florida writer of that name. In the 1990s Lunch resumed a working relationship with poet and singer Exene Cervenka, formerly of X, on a spoken word CD *Rude Hieroglyphics*. Together they had previously published a collection of poems, *Adulterers Anonymous*, through Grove Press (1982). In addition she has run a visiting artists workshop in San Francisco, and exhibited her photographs, body artworks (consisting of variously rendered casts of her body) and voodoo boxes round America.

"Am I less angry than I was at 13?" Lunch concludes. "No. Am I more angry? No. Am I more aware? Yes."

Chris Bohn

Creation Books International
http://www.pussycat.demon.co.uk
UK office:
83, Clerkenwell Road, London EC1R 5AR
Tel: 0171-430-9878 Fax: 0171-242-5527
E-mail: creation@pussycat.demon.co.uk
US office:
173 Slater Boulevard, Staten Island, NY 10305
Tel: 718-351-9599 Fax: 718-980-4262
E-mail: MKPubServ@aol.com
Creation products should be available in all proper bookstores; please ask your local retailer to order from:
UK & Europe: Turnaround Distribution, Unit 3 Olympia Trading Estate, Coburg Road, Wood Green, London N22 6TZ
Tel: 0181-829-3000 Fax: 0181-881-5088
Italy: Apeiron Editoria & Distribuzione, Piazza Orazio Moroni 4, 00060 Sant'Oreste (Roma)
Tel: 0761-579670 Fax: 0761-579737
USA: Subterranean Company, Box 160, 265 South 5th Street, Monroe, OR 97456
Tel: 503 847-5274 Fax: 503-847-6018
US Non-Book Trade: Last Gasp, 777 Florida Street, San Francisco, CA 94110-0682
Tel: 415-824-6636 Fax: 415-824-1836
Canada: Marginal, Unit 102, 277 George Street, N. Peterborough, Ontario K9J 3G9
Tel/Fax: 705-745-2326
Australia & NZ: Peribo Pty Ltd, 58 Beaumont Road, Mount Kuring-gai, NSW 2080
Tel: 02-457-0011 Fax: 02-457-0022
Japan: Tuttle-Shokai, 21-13 Seki 1-Chome, Tama-ku, Kawasaki, Kanagawa 214
Tel: 44-833-1924 Fax: 44-833-7559

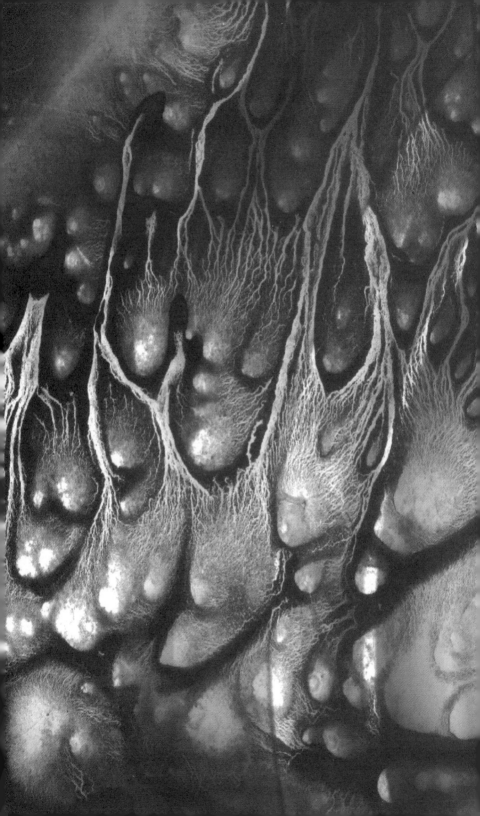